The Simian King spit its last vicious roar at us—but that was no longer enough to scare me and my friends.

"You've underestimated humans for the last time, Your Royal Monkeyness."

Arihito's Party

Job: Rearguard
The story's protagonist. Currently making waves in his mysterious support-based job.

Arihito Atobe

Job: Rogue
A demi-human girl and Arihito's first party member.

Theresia

Job: Valkyrie
Formerly Arihito's boss, now she's his biggest advocate.

Kyouka Igarashi

Job: Flawless Knight
A skilled swordfighter working with the party to rescue her close friend.

Elitia Centrale

Job: Shrine Maiden
A reserved young girl who supports the party with her bow and arrow and other special skills.

Suzuna Shiromiya

Job: Gambler
Capable of tweaking the odds in battle. The party's personal cheerleader.

Misaki Nitou

Job: Merchant
The party's lifeline, fully responsible for stocking and transporting their supplies.

Madoka Shinonogi

Job: Dissector
Highly adept at dissections despite her youth. Her mother is a demi-human.

Melissa Rikerton

Job: Silver Hound
A guard dog on the party's front line. Very close with Kyouka.

Cion

Job: Riot Soldier
Steadfast Guild Savior offering Arihito and his party stopgap support.

Seraphina Edelbert

The WORLD'S STRONGEST REARGUARD | Labyrinth Country's Novice Seeker

8

Tôwa

Illustration by **Huuka Kazabana**

Translation by Alexandra McCullough-Garcia and John Neal
Cover art by Huuka Kazabana

SEKAI SAIKYO NO KOEI -MEIKYUKOKU NO SHINJIN TANSAKUSHA- Volume 8
©Tôwa, Huuka Kazabana 2021
First published in Japan in 2021 by KADOKAWA CORPORATION, Tokyo.
English translation rights arranged with KADOKAWA CORPORATION, Tokyo through
TUTTLE-MORI AGENCY, INC., Tokyo.

Yen On
150 West 30th Street, 19th Floor
New York, NY 10001

Visit us at yenpress.com
facebook.com/yenpress
twitter.com/yenpress
yenpress.tumblr.com
instagram.com/yenpress

First Yen On Edition: June 2023
Edited by Yen On Editorial: Rachel Mimms
Designed by Yen Press Design: Andy Swist

Yen On is an imprint of Yen Press, LLC.
The Yen On name and logo are trademarks of Yen Press, LLC.

Library of Congress Cataloging-in-Publication Data
Names: Tôwa, author. | Kazabana, Huuka, illustrator. | Taylor, Jordan (Translator), translator. |
    McCullough-Garcia, Alexandra (Translator), translator.
Title: The world's strongest rearguard: labyrinth country's novice seeker / Tôwa ; illustration by
    Huuka Kazabana.
Other titles: Sekai saikyo no koei: meikyukoku no shinjin tansakusha. English
Description: First Yen On edition. | New York, NY : Yen ON, 2019– | v. 1–4 Translator,
    Jordan Taylor — v. 5–6 Translator, Alexandra McCullough-Garcia.
Identifiers: LCCN 2019030466 | ISBN 9781975331542 (v. 1 ; trade paperback) |
    ISBN 9781975331566 (v. 2 ; trade paperback) | ISBN 9781975331580 (v. 3 ; trade paperback) |
    ISBN 9781975315719 (v. 4 ; trade paperback) | ISBN 9781975315733 (v. 5 ; trade paperback) |
    ISBN 9781975333331 (v. 6 ; trade paperback) | ISBN 9781975343934 (v. 7 ; trade paperback) |
    ISBN 9781975350550 (v. 8 ; trade paperback)
Subjects: CYAC: Fantasy. | Future life—Fiction.
Classification: LCC PZ7.1.T676 Wo 2019 | DDC [Fic]—dc23
LC record available at https://lccn.loc.gov/2019030466

ISBNs: 978-1-9753-5055-0 (paperback)
        978-1-9753-5056-7 (ebook)

10 9 8 7 6 5 4 3 2 1

LSC-C

Printed in the United States of America

CONTENTS

Little did we know when Falma opened the Black Box we'd acquired from The Calamity that the Hidden God part within would forcibly teleport us to a lost labyrinth. Waiting for us there was the master of the labyrinth, the Intelligent Armor Fylgja; as we had with Murakumo and Alphecca, we fought fiercely and just barely came out of the battle victorious.

We did not, however, have to destroy Fylgja to do so. In fact, it was Fylgja herself who accepted defeat before we dealt the final blow. I then affixed the Merak Crystal, an armament controller, onto her armor and gained official ownership of another Hidden God part.

In her materialized form, Fylgja looked like a female knight, although her figure was semitransparent from fatigue. She briefly introduced herself to Murakumo and Alphecca and then once again knelt before me.

"Master Arihito, I can be equipped as armor during expeditions much like Murakumo; alternatively, I can release my physical form and travel with you."

"So we can call you to us like Alphecca?"

"Aye. However, this means I can also be lost during emergency evacuation from a labyrinth, whether via a Hidden God's provenance or a Return Scroll."

"Does that mean we'll lose something when we get out of here, too?"

"Nay. Anyone who defeats me may exit this labyrinth through the teleportation circle that lies ahead; if you proceed via this route, nothing will be taken from you."

I guess that means we can get out of here if we just keep going forward.

Perhaps moved with sorrow for the Seekers who'd lost their lives to Fylgja, Suzuna, who had turned back to face the way we had come, was praying. I followed her example, putting my hand over my heart and closing my eyes.

"Hidden God parts are duty bound to test Seekers... But why is that, Fylgja...?" asked Igarashi.

Fylgja, who preferred to answer in terms of aye or nay, said neither.

"That is how we are created," she replied. "Until we submit to an armament controller, we engage every soul that comes to us in a test of strength that ends with either our destruction or the will of the Hidden God devotee we thereafter serve."

"Hmm. I've got mixed feelings on this, but I guess you're someone we want on our side...," Misaki mused. "Also, all you parts ladies are super-pretty. And now you're here like a super-cool knight in shining armor."

"I am no knightly suit of armor. When equipped by either a Seeker or a Hidden God, I more closely resemble an additional layer of protection," Fylgja responded in all seriousness, striking a very knightly figure indeed.

While similar in some regards to Seraphina's equipment, Fylgja did seem less like a typical suit of armor and more like a futuristic protector you might see in a sci-fi film.

Soon enough, Fylgja's form began fading, providing glimpses of the scenery behind her.

"Fylgja, you're starting to disappear. Are you low on magic?" I asked.

"Aye. After a certain degree of movement, I require additional magic to sustain my material form."

"It would behoove us to regard Fylgja as a secret layer of protection anyone can call upon in times of need, as we do not need to specify a single Seeker to equip her," said Murakumo. "Hmm, it seems I have also overspent my magic."

Murakumo in her physical manifestation nodded in agreement with Alphecca and Fylgja, then looked at me. I nodded back, and the three women vanished into thin air.

"…First a blade, then a chariot, and now I reclaim a frame. This is all thanks to your support, Arihito, and that of your friends," I heard Ariadne say.

I took that opportunity to ask about something on my mind. "Ariadne, you've had the Guard Arm from the beginning, right? Is that also a Hidden God part?"

"My mechanical arm is a section of my equipment that is unique to me. This varies among every Hidden God."

"I see... It's very like you to have a Guard Arm, one that's protected us all."

Though all I had to do was imagine the words for them to reach Ariadne, I heard nothing from her for a while.

Did I say something to make her uncomfortable?

"It is a Hidden God's duty to bestow their protection on their devotees. If I have succeeded in this task, then I am glad of it."

"You always do. Thank you. What will happen if we keep collecting more of your parts?"

"...Not even I know the answer. Much of the knowledge I once possessed was lost when I was disposed of," she admitted. "Of one thing I am certain: The number of parts I have reclaimed will play a vital role in the event that we cross paths with a hostile god of my kind."

Though Ariadne had warned us of that from the beginning, we had yet to run into any "hostile Hidden Gods."

"...I cannot say anything for certain, but ever since you ascended to your current district, I have felt slightly on edge. However, I pray you merely take note of this, as it has no logical basis."

"Meaning...we might face an enemy Hidden God in District Five, right? I sure hope we can hold off on that until after our battle with the Simian Lord."

"As do I. The Simian Lord is a formidable foe, and its vanquishing will prove a challenging feat. All I can do is prepare to protect the lives of my devotees on the day of battle," she said, a tinge of undeniable emotion coloring her once robotically mechanical voice. Her promise to protect us gave me more heart than I could ever have asked for. "...*Perhaps using the Shrine Maiden as a conduit has affected me some.*"

"O-oh... *Yeah, you might be right.*"

"I'm more than happy to use Medium again. We need it to bolster your protection over us, don't we?"

Suzuna, who had returned to stand by me before I knew it and apparently could also hear what Ariadne had been saying, chimed in.

"*I cannot fathom how our conversation inspired a desire to utilize that skill.*"

"I beg your pardon. It's just, last time I got to thinking perhaps it would be best to do so regularly, but we haven't had a chance since then..."

"R-right, Ariadne does get stronger the more our devotion grows, after all. I agree with you, we really should raise our devotion levels again like we did before."

"*...If that is your intention, then I cannot refuse. The session should go quickly enough that it will not impede your rest.*"

That seemed enough to earn Ariadne's permission and portended our first Medium session in a while later that evening.

We found the transportation circle and returned to where we'd been. Just then—

"Oh, thank goodness, you're all—!"

"Fo—! Fa-Fahma, I can'h breahe…!" choked Misaki, who reappeared closest to Falma and instantly found herself buried in the Chest Cracker's bosom.

Not one to stare, I quickly averted my gaze; my eyes fell on Igarashi, who for some reason also looked away.

"D-don't tell me…you want *me* to h-hold you like that, Atobe," she stammered.

"Oh, n-no, I, um…"

"…Kyouka, you're telling on yourself."

"…M-Melissa, I wasn't saying— Eek!"

"I'm *so* glad you're all okay…! I never stopped praying you'd be all right…!"

Madoka flung her arms around Igarashi from behind, rejoicing in our safe return. But before I could join in the celebration, I had to figure out how much time had passed while we were gone. The flow of time was known to vary depending on where we teleported.

"Sorry to worry you, Madoka… How long did it take for us to get back?"

"I-it's okay! Umm… The sun has already set, so I think you were away for about six hours."

The air had been similarly dry where we found Alphecca and now Fylgja. Clearly, the quicker the weathering took its toll, the faster time flew.

"We were fortunate not to have lost a significant number of

hours there," said Seraphina. "I suggest we tackle opening the next Black Box tomorrow and allow ourselves some rest."

"Yes, that's probably best."

She's got a good point; we should call it a day.

No sooner had the thought crossed my mind than Misaki finally freed herself from Falma's embrace and walked over to me.

"Falma, I'm sorry to have caused you so much grief," I said.

"Oh, no... I'd worried at first that I'd failed at opening the chest, but this one felt somehow different. A true failure could have made everything in this room vanish entirely."

"...Wow, chest cracking is really risky. Sorry for pushing all these difficult treasure boxes on you."

"There's no need to apologize; I am a professional, for what it's worth, and I find great meaning in helping crack chests," Falma insisted. "If this was indeed a success, I do hope you will trust me again in the future with your treasure box needs."

She then bowed. I'd been careful to avoid watching her bend over at all, but the downward-then-upward movement was exponentially more risqué—my eyes found no safe landing in sight.

"......"

"Theresia, looks like Ari-poo really does love the busty ladies."

"......!"

"H-hey. Let's try to keep on topic here..."

"Forgive me; I've been so worried this whole time I didn't have a chance to change...," Falma admitted. "I think I may need to avail myself of your bath."

The intense concentration of cracking a chest always left Falma dripping in sweat.

Maybe that's why she's glowing now, too— Wait, now's not the time for that.

"Falma, could we ask you to help us with the remaining Black Box tomorrow?" I asked.

"Yes, of course. A good night's sleep will restore all the energy I need to have another go."

Our order-made wagon should be ready tomorrow; we'll also need to head out in search of a Holy Stone to fashion a Curse Eater blade. Opening that last Black Box does run the risk of putting us up against another Hidden God part, but considering it could also give us new equipment, that's a risk we should take sooner rather than later.

Falma was undoubtedly one of the great pillars supporting our party behind the scenes. I also knew, however, that asking for her help meant taking her away from Eyck and Plum. With all that in mind, I decided I wanted to find some way to thank her—I simply had to.

After first dropping by the apartment suite, I headed to see Ceres and Steiner at the workshop. There I was greeted by the sight of Steiner working on an organ that had been removed from The Calamity; they seemed to be connecting tubes.

"Oh, welcome back!"

"The operation to remove the Queen's Tail from the Queen Scorpion went swimmingly. All that is now left is to power it with magic for a test run," Ceres informed me. "We must take every precaution."

Made from materials we'd harvested from The Calamity, the Queen's Tail was something like a large arterial weapon too heavy for any one person to wield. However, we were hoping we could manage to use it if we loaded it onto a cart Madoka could operate.

"Thank you very much. I'm sorry to interrupt while you're already so busy, but we just opened a Black Box, and I was hoping to discuss some items we found... Seraphina's armor was also damaged, so I'd like to ask you to repair that as well."

"I'm quite sure we can handle a few additional repairs and process whatever items you gathered from the treasure chest without trouble," Ceres said. "Now, let me see what we have here."

Madoka, who had accompanied me to the workshop, used her skill Unpack Goods to retrieve our newest acquisitions: Water Serpent Scales and the ripped Heavenly Maiden's Raiment. The Ice Remnant had also dropped a frost stone, but I decided to hold on to it for use as bullets with my magical gun.

"This raiment...no, you shan't be able to use it in this state; it's much too tattered. Steiner and I could wash it for you, but any repairs would be beyond us."

"*Maybe a skilled tailor could fix it for you?*" Steiner ventured. "*Oh, I know! Luca could definitely help.*"

"True, he is a professional, after all. I'll try reaching out to him at Boutique Corleone down in District Seven," Madoka said as she started jotting down a to-do list in her notebook.

Just as I was wondering what we might do with the Water Serpent Scales, Steiner stepped away from their work, walked over to us, and picked up one of the scales.

"I can feel the scale's water power just by holding it in my hand. This resource will be better as armor than as a weapon."

"About that—do you think you could add it to the wagon we're having made now once it's ready?"

"As a defensive shield? A fine idea, I should say; simply affixing a scale will improve the wagon's heat resistance, after all. You could add multiple if you like, but with this quality, I imagine one should do quite nicely."

"If you put it at the head of the wagon, it'll react to flames and create a film around the entire vehicle," Steiner informed me. *"That will take magical power from whoever is riding it, though."*

Following that plan, we would have two remaining scales to use on equipment. As neither Elitia nor Melissa, who took on quite a bit of attacking duty as well, had fire attribute–resistant armor, I decided to have Ceres and Steiner strengthen their equipment.

"Though Elitia's High Mithril Knightmail has reached its fortification limit, we can temporarily bolster it by adding the Water Serpent Scale as supplementary armor. However, pushing past that limit would require special materials, so I suggest you consider switching to an entirely new piece of equipment instead."

"That's great advice, thank you. What about Melissa's armor?"

"Well, I do believe it best to apply the scales to a piece that covers most of her body. Her White Apocynum Overalls can be fortified up to +6; this would leave them at +1, with plenty of room for further modifications."

I guess since all equipment has a cap on modifications, we should upgrade to better base armor any chance we get. If we want to aim for the strongest armor possible, we should use only the resources we harvest from the strongest monsters we defeat.

"Collecting a complete set of armor is quite the challenge, you see. If you find a suitable set that can be used as is, it would behoove you to switch to that. You also have the option of extracting the attributes and modifications you've made to the previous items, leaving the original piece."

"Is that even possible? That's amazing."

"My profession is well suited to the task, in fact. That woman... Lynée, that is, also does similar work, though through different means," Ceres explained. "The method I use converts and then extracts the capabilities imbued in a piece of equipment."

She brought over the tricorn cap she often wore, then whispered a spell that brought letters floating to the surface.

"I added this power to my hat, but it will vanish if I simply remove it. The feat can be accomplished with what is known as a transmitter pearl, though I have not seen one these last few years. They can only be used a certain number of times and are only ever rarely found in labyrinths."

"A transmitter pearl... That's good to know. I'll keep it in mind."

"Arihito, I'll check if I can find one through Bargain," Madoka piped up.

"Great. Keep an eye on its market price, too. I imagine it can get pretty pricey, but it's probably worth it."

"We'll go over to pick up the items you need repaired or processed, okay? We should have them done by morning."

"I can't thank you enough. We'll have a good meal tonight— and please make sure to take breaks."

"Mm, I must say, I am quite looking forward to trying the cuisine in this district; each one boasts different styles, after all," noted Ceres. "Now then, shall we see what we can do before dinner?"

"Yes, Master."

"Oh, I think I'll go make some tea. Is that okay, Arihito?" Madoka asked.

Such a conscientious girl. I was thinking to do that myself, but maybe it's best to delegate. While she's busy with that, I'll go get the things we need to leave with Steiner and Ceres.

Once night fell, it was off to the Forest Diner. We found it cheerfully bustling as always, with Seekers congratulating each other on another hard day's work and sharing drinks.

The hostess instructed us to once again head for the meeting room that also functioned as a private dining area, where apparently Maria would be serving us once more. We had originally agreed the Chef would deliver the dishes she prepared with our special fruits to our place, but Madoka had arranged for her to give them to us here.

"……"

Theresia looked curious about what the other diners were enjoying, but still she kept following behind me.

…Hmm?

Suddenly, a hush seemed to fall over the area—conversations still continued, but with lowered voices. All the diners around us focused their attention on one area. Elitia, who had been walking with Suzuna and Misaki, also stopped short when she saw the band of people approaching us: the White Night Brigade. I saw one group led by Vice Captain Agnes, and another walking in front of it. The young man with a bluish tint in his black hair in the center of this latter group stopped at the sight of us, then used his middle finger to push up his glasses.

"…Captain…Johan…," Elitia whispered, just as I caught up to and stepped in front of her. The young man she'd called Johan ambled toward us, grinning.

Ice cold—that was the first impression I got as I met his gaze. Whatever emotions lurked behind those clear blue eyes didn't easily fit into one simple category.

"Didn't think I'd run into you here. I was sure I'd see you at some point, but it looks like that came quicker than I'd expected."

"…Captain, Elitia is now—"

"Working with another party," Johan said, interrupting Agnes. "I understand... Elitia, I know I didn't stop you when you set off on your own. But that doesn't mean I've given up on you."

"...!"

He closed in on Elitia and extended his right hand to her. But a handshake was the last thing on his mind.

"...Would you show me the sword? I'd like to see if you've made any progress since you left."

The sword in question, the Scarlet Emperor, had recently awakened to its true power and reclaimed its true name, Antares. As long as it stayed within its scabbard, though, the blade's transformation remained our secret.

Elitia had been assigned the Scarlet Emperor back when she still belonged to the Brigade. I saw absolutely no signs that Johan understood exactly how much suffering that had caused her. However, precisely because the Brigade had given Elitia a sword they'd acquired, there remained the possibility they would push their claim to it. And if we lost Antares now, we would lose almost any chance we had of defeating the Simian Lord.

"Afraid I can't. I'm still not ready to give it back."

"...Do you still mean to take down that ape? That monster has mastered the art of forcing humans into servitude. If you lose, you'll end up just like her...like that Healer," Johan pressed, not even calling Rury by name.

Agnes kept her gaze firmly on the floor. Most of the other Brigade members simply listened in on the conversation, completely dispassionate.

"I don't much like the idea of my own flesh and blood sister becoming some ape's minion. If you haven't mastered that sword, I'd like to take it back while I have you here."

"...Captain, that's a bit much...," Agnes protested.

"This is a family matter," Johan insisted. "You must understand, Ellie. I didn't give you that blade for you to deliver it into the hands of a monster."

Clearly, he didn't believe we could defeat the Simian Lord or bring Rury back safely.

I knew Johan was Elitia's elder brother, but the details of how their family had been reincarnated in the Labyrinth Country or of the kind of relationships they had were still mostly a mystery to me. Even so, my companions and I did know one thing: the reason Elitia had pushed herself so hard, what she had risked her life for.

"Elitia is part of my party now," I said. "We have important business to take care of. As Elitia's family, I wish you wouldn't disparage her goals."

"Arihito..."

I turned to face Johan head-on; my skin crawled, a warning that I'd stepped into my opponent's territory. As a group, the Brigade strove to collect cursed weapons in pursuit of their awesome power. While I couldn't tell exactly what went on in the mind of the one leading that charge, I did feel an oppressive power emanating from the sword at his waist that told me it was no ordinary weapon.

"Arihito...is it? You find my sister's sword appealing?"

"Not just her sword. Elitia's a vital member of our party."

"No one could ever take Ellie's place," said Igarashi. "We've come all this way fighting side by side, supporting each other, putting our hearts and souls into our work...and we intend to keep things that way."

Johan studied Igarashi with amusement, but that hardly compared to the intense stares the other male members of his party focused on her.

"D-damn... What a fox... You don't see goods like that every day."

"You say that every time you see a woman with a big rack, Souga."

"Forget that for a second. Am I seeing things, or is that guy in the suit the only dude in that whole group...? Talk about a lady killer. It's always the quiet-looking ones who get all the chicks...!"

"Silence, Jeremy. You make yourself look like a fool whenever you open your mouth."

Souga, it seemed, hadn't gotten a good look at Igarashi the last time he'd seen her. As soon as she noticed the other men leering at her, Igarashi retreated behind me. I could almost feel their stares boring holes into me, but my place now was protecting Igarashi.

"...If you've yet to awaken the blade, I'm willing to give you some more time. But...," Johan began.

Just then, his eyes flew open wide in realization. He smiled. He wasn't looking at me, though; his gaze was fixed on something far in the distance.

"I see… So that's how it is. Well, that's fine. No need to rush…"

"…Captain, we're just as much to blame for leaving Rury behind. Can we not help Elitia in some way?"

"If you fail, you'll have to clean up the mess. That's always been my stance, Agnes."

"…!"

Agnes was trying to go against Johan's wishes and lend us a hand. That said, it would be nearly impossible to come back from a battle against the Simian Lord unscathed. What Johan had told her essentially amounted to a direct order not to help us in any way.

"I had not expected to see you here, and for now I've had my fill. Let's meet again, Elitia—if you survive."

"…Wait. Johan, is Father—?"

"He's alive. But I am the captain now. I suggest you don't hold on to hopes for his help."

And with that, the Brigade left the Forest Diner. They were fifteen strong, enough to fill two parties, counting Johan. A variety of vanguards, middle guards, and rearguards, the group consisted of eight men and seven women.

Elitia didn't turn back to watch them; for a moment, she kept her eyes on the floor. Eventually, she looked up and gave Suzuna and Misaki at her side a smile.

"Don't worry," she told them. "I've known what kind of person my brother is for a long time. It's no shock to me now."

"…Oh, good. I'm so happy to see you smile, Ellie."

"I thought he'd have this harsh exterior with a warm, squishy filling, but…he wasn't anything like that. Kinda scary…," Misaki mused. "Ack! I shouldn't say that about your brother…"

"…He didn't always speak about my father like that. One day, it was like he became a completely different person… But I don't know anything about why."

Despite the cold impression he left, Johan apparently used to be different. Something must have happened after he came to the Labyrinth Country to turn him into the man he was today.

"Ms. Agnes seemed genuinely concerned for us. However, I imagine asking for help the way matters stand now will not earn us much."

"Good point, Seraphina," I said. "Still, that means not everyone in the Brigade sees us as enemies…and I'm grateful for that, at least."

Seraphina, who'd told us ahead of time she'd come a little late, joined our conversation. Rikerton bashfully approached, his wife Ferris in tow.

"Arihito, there's something I'd like to ask you… Would it be all right if my wife Feresia joined us?"

So Ferris is a nickname for Feresia?

I smiled. "Of course. It would be our pleasure to have you both again."

"…Meow."

"……"

As a lizardman, Theresia couldn't speak at all, while Ferris, a werecat, was able to meow. The two of them appeared to be communicating somehow.

"...Looks like Theresia can understand my mom. Amazing... Even I only get the gist of it."

Melissa gazed at them fondly; she rarely showed an expression like that. I got the impression that being with her mother had inspired a positive change in Melissa, a development that made me as happy as if it had been my own.

CHAPTER 1

Precious Little Time, New Equipment

Part I: A Pleasant Chat and Three Types of Dessert

Though our unexpected meeting with Johan and the White Night Brigade had left us all tense, my party and I shook it off and headed to the Forest Diner's private dining area with Rikerton's family as well as Louisa, Ceres, and Steiner. We split into two groups and took our seats at the two tables; soon after, a man and a woman came to take our drink orders.

"Atobe, are you having something to drink?"

"I think that could help us all relax a little. What do you say we forget about coordinating and just order whatever we like for a toast?"

"I have to thank you, Arihito. My wife's taken a liking to silverline wine ever since she became a werecat, and apparently they serve it here."

Ferris looked at Rikerton and twitched her ears, clearly a sign of agreement. I'd had no idea, but evidently Ferris's acute sense of smell had alerted her to the wine in the establishment.

"...I want to try some," said Melissa. "Am I too young?"

"...Meowww."

"Ha-ha...," Rikerton chuckled. "Well, your mom seems to be saying that you should do as you please. Personally, I think you're a bit young for a drink."

"Oh...okay. I'll have juice, then," Melissa replied, readily capitulating to her father's wishes.

Ferris, seated at Melissa's side, silently began stroking her hair. Melissa looked embarrassed, but nonetheless happy.

"Let's see... I'll have this District Five specialty, the aqua-blue wine, please," I said.

"Excellent choice. This comes in a small pitcher that serves about ten cups."

"I might as well have that too," Igarashi chimed in. "It's alcoholic, but the menu says it won't leave a hangover."

"Ooh, then maybe we should get ourselves a little pitcher of that, huh, Suzu?" said Misaki. "Juuust kidding. I'll have this refreshing mint juice."

"I'll have that as well, please," Suzuna added.

As the rest of our party continued ordering their drinks, I showed the menu to Theresia, who was sitting next to me, so she could choose what she wanted. After studying the list for a minute, she decided on the mixed fruit juice.

"......"

Nothing about Theresia seemed out of the ordinary, but I couldn't keep myself from stealing sideways glances at her. Igarashi saw this from across the table and whispered, "I'm sure we'll make it in time. Try not to torment yourself too much, Atobe."

"You're right, thank you. I'll be fine."

I'd take Theresia's place in an instant if I could. She's always gotten us out of the nastiest scrapes in the nick of time. Maybe that's why somewhere deep inside I've been clinging to her as a ray of hope.

Our drinks were soon rolled into the room on a wagon. Once everyone had their own glass in hand, we asked Rikerton to lead us in a toast.

"If I hadn't met Arihito in District Eight, I wouldn't be here with my wife and daughter tonight. I'd like to propose a toast of renewed thanks for that blessing… From the bottom of my heart, and with gratitude for the opportunity to be with you all here this evening, I'd also like to raise our glasses to safe passage throughout your seeking. Cheers!"

""""Cheers!""""

I took a swig from the pint glass Theresia had filled for me with my wine; it was an absolute delight, entirely different from any other wine I'd had before, with sweet and refreshingly tart tones that went down like a dream.

"Mm…!" Igarashi murmured. "It goes down so nice. I wonder why all the drinks in the Labyrinth Country are this delicious."

"The effects of this wine do not linger for long, but it will nonetheless catch up to you. Please do indulge in moderation," the server who had brought us our drinks politely advised.

Igarashi and Louisa looked at each other.

"R-really?" asked Igarashi. "I sort of just threw it back..."

"I must admit I did as well...," Louisa added.

"Well, holding out can be pretty taxing, too. Please, have as much as you like," I reassured them, then drained about half of my glass.

It probably wasn't the most common way to enjoy wine, but the aqua-blue wine went down so nicely, I felt I could drink it as easily as water.

Next to come out were our hors d'oeuvres, which everyone munched away at to their heart's content. Ferris was feeding Rikerton a few morsels; I gathered that must have been their custom back when they still lived together. It was an intimate scene, one that left me feeling a bit like a voyeur.

"Guess you would love fish, wouldn't you?" Misaki joked. "...Are you gonna be okay with that silverline wine?"

"Melissa, you look a little red...," said Suzuna.

Melissa wasn't supposed to have had any of the feline-friendly wine, but Misaki and Suzuna made a fair point. Even from a distance, I could see Melissa's face was a little flushed. Although, to be fair, even the slightest tinge of red stood out sharply against her snow-white skin.

"...*Hic*. Mom, have a bite of this."

"Meooow."

"Young Rikerton, I understand this must be a happy reunion for you, but perhaps you can think of the place it has put us in these two nights," Ceres teased.

"Ha-ha-ha, you got me there... I'd thought for sure I would not see this day for a long while yet to come, so happy as a clam I am, indeed."

"Ferris, you seem thinner than the last time I saw you... And am I imagining things, or have you done something with your fur?" Falma asked.

Clearly, she and Ferris were already acquaintances. The two mothers seemed to share a special connection that enveloped their whole table in warmth.

"Apparently, one of my wife's skills as a werecat gives her the ability to change the color of her fur."

"Then maybe mine will change, too. I inherited her same skills, so...*hic*."

"*Melissa, are you all right? Why don't you have a nice glass of water and drink slowly?*" Steiner helpfully suggested, but Melissa's hiccups didn't seem to be going anywhere.

I'd been in her shoes before, so I started getting a little worried. Or, rather, I started to wonder whether she wasn't in fact drunk on the silverline wine.

"Oh, I know how to stop hiccups! You just drink from the opposite side of the cup, like this!"

"Misaki, you shouldn't shoot out of your seat like that...," chided Suzuna.

"My grandmother showed me a few tricks for how to get rid of hiccups," Madoka added.

Soon all three girls had gotten up from their seats. We were free to move around as we liked, so before long, Seraphina left her seat and came to our table.

"Excellent work today, Mr. Atobe."

"Likewise. Thank you."

Sensing Seraphina was about to refill my glass, I drained what was left of the wine. She wound up topping it off once more to the brim, but I figured I could handle this much.

"I wanted to speak to you about Fylgja. Ever since she dematerialized, she's been communicating with me."

"Oh, she has...? What's she been saying to you?"

"She was curious about my experience as the person responsible for frontline defenses. I believe I managed to share the knowledge I have, but she seemed quite surprised and noted we have a tendency to fight monsters much stronger than our party level."

"Hard to argue with that...," Igarashi agreed. "You and Ellie are more on par with those monsters, while the rest of us bring down the party's overall average."

"Charging in alone isn't actually a great way to contribute to a party," said Elitia. "Arihito always finds a way to make me feel included. That's why I'll never go off on my own again."

Elitia seemed to be warning herself with her repeated admissions of remorse, but I for one couldn't see her making the same mistake twice.

"Forget that for a sec, Ellie," said Misaki. "You see, our little Suzuna here..."

"...Wh-what?"

"You haven't had a bite yet... Here, say *aah*," Suzuna instructed as she fed Elitia an appetizer.

"Ngh...! *Gulp*... Th-thanks...," Elitia replied shyly. Suzuna smiled, content.

The next instant, Misaki popped up behind me. "Arihitooo, Theresia looks like she wants in on the fun. Will you let her? Okay, it's a done deal!"

"Uh, b-but we're already—"

"......"

Theresia cut off a piece of my fish, skewered it on her fork, and offered it to me. The white-meat fish glazed with a perfectly tart vinegar sauce melted so wonderfully in my mouth, I felt my cheeks soften all on their own.

"C'mon, Arihito, you know it's only polite to return the favor, right? The technical term for it is a 'cross-counter.'"

"A little bit on the nose, that term, but she's not wrong."

"N-not you, too, Igarashi... *Ahem*. Theresia, may I?"

Nodding, Theresia turned toward me. She had already started eating on her own, and now licked her lips clean with her tiny tongue.

"*Theresia's tongue is so cute...*," thought Arihito.

The narration came courtesy of Misaki, of course, but for once I couldn't deny her claim. Meanwhile, Theresia waited for me with her mouth open. Everyone's focus was trained on me, and I fed her a morsel in return.

"...Mmn..."

"Hoo boy, nope, that's way too shmexy. There you go again, Arihito, working us up without even realizing it. And now I'm gonna be the one to pay for it. If I can't sleep at all tonight, I'm gonna—"

"Misaki, I suggest you rein it in or the rest of us will have to do it for you," Igarashi cut in. "But also…Atobe, you shouldn't be giving Misaki any more fodder."

"N-no, that wasn't my intention…"

"…There'll be no end to it if I start asking you to fulfill my own selfish desires now, so I do hope you'll excuse me for seconding Kyouka's rebuke."

"What—? I—I mean, *I'm* okay, but don't let me stop *you*, Louisa."

"…Are you quite sure?"

Before I knew it, things at my table had gotten really tense.

What should I do? As their leader, is it my job to give everyone a warning?

"And now, your meat dishes. Today we have skewers of the Chef's inspiration."

There wasn't much room for turning it down if the Chef—in other words, Maria—had planned this dish herself, was there? Perfect finger food, skewers made for easy hand-feeding.

"And the race is on to see who can get more in Arihito before he's totally full…or…"

But before Misaki could finish her declaration, Theresia had already picked up a skewer and held it out for me. Explaining in my defense to no one in particular that grilled meat and spices brought out our most primitive urges, I took a bite. Theresia studied me closely as if to see whether I liked it. All I could do was smile and give her a thumbs-up.

The diner had also prepared a special guard dog dish for Cion, which Falma was now feeding her.

"She's become quite dependable, hasn't she?" Falma noted. "She's only a little bigger than when we had her at home, but there's something more mature about her now."

"Cion's been a tremendous help. She not only keeps our party safe, she also rescues townspeople when there's a crisis..."

Falma pressed her forehead against Cion's, then turned to me with a smile. "Whenever I do this, I can feel what she feels. Call it an owner's intuition."

"Wow..."

"Hee-hee..." She chuckled. "That said, all I can really discern is that she's quite taken with you, Mr. Atobe."

"Woof!"

"...Th-that tickles... What's gotten into you?"

As if she'd understood Falma, Cion stopped lapping up water and licked my cheek.

"Please take her wherever your journey takes you, Mr. Atobe. I will always be happy to have her at home as well, if you think she needs a rest."

"Thank you, Falma. But I think Cion's home will always be with you and your children..."

"...My owner's intuition also tells me what Cion wants most to do now, what she treasures most."

What Cion wants... If what she wants is to be part of our party, then I need to think extra carefully to make sure she doesn't get hurt and avoid pitting her against dangerous monsters.

"Mr. Atobe, guard dogs are a proud breed. They want you to believe in their strength. This little one's mother, Astarte, was exactly the same."

Cion was sitting obediently, watching me with eyes that seemed to see right through my concerns and tell me I had no need to worry.

"Cion, want to keep pushing forward with us?"

"Arf!"

"C'mon, Atobe, stop hogging Cion all to yourself..."

"My apologies, Kyouka. Cion, go have Kyouka give you a few pets."

"...Y-you sure? Who's a good girl...?"

Cion had also grown quite attached to Igarashi, who was returning that love with much less inhibition now, thanks perhaps to a little liquid courage. The guard dog's face buried in her chest, Igarashi scratched and petted her canine friend to her heart's content.

"...Mr. Atobe, would you care to follow Cion's example?"

"My, my... It looks like you're feeling rather bold yourself, Louisa. What would you say to another drink with me?" Falma asked.

"Of course, gladly... Mr. Atobe, won't you join us, too?"

Though it wasn't my place to say, tipsy Louisa was terrifyingly sexy. With her clothes slightly disheveled and her hair down, loose of its usual buns, she had more than enough mature appeal to go around.

"Pardon the interruption, but…Mr. Atobe, may I have a word?"

"S-sure. What's this about, Maria?"

With impeccable timing, my savior—or rather, Maria—brought over the desserts I had asked her to bake.

"This is a soufflé made from the Herculean Walnuts and freshly harvested labyrinth pears. With the Apples of Wit I baked an apple pie, and I used the Nimble Grapes to make a fruit syrup to be enjoyed drizzled over pancakes."

Maria placed the desserts on our table. Each one looked like a delicacy served at a first-rate restaurant. There were three soufflés, four slices of apple pie, and three servings of pancakes. Our supporting artisans and staff received other desserts as well.

"One of my skills allows me to spread the effects of one ingredient over two or three dishes. Once you partake of one power-granting ingredient, there is a window of time during which you will not be able to feel the effects of anything else, so eating more than one will not grant any more benefits."

"But there are enough desserts here so we can all feel some benefit…correct? Thank you very much, Maria."

"Smells sooo sweet… There's always room for dessert…"

"Y-yeah… I have to agree with you there, Misaki. But is it really okay for us to have something this valuable…?" Suzuna wondered.

"It's going to be hard to choose one…," I noted. "Seraphina, which will you have?"

"Hmm… A particularly difficult question, indeed. Perhaps the soufflé…but then again, it is hard to pass up the apple pie… Hah!"

"The power boost is one aspect, but it gets even trickier when you think of which type of dessert you want... Atobe, what are you going for?"

Perhaps stymied by a general love of desserts, we were all finding it hard to pick our pleasure. However, we couldn't leave Rikerton and the others waiting forever, so I bit the bullet and made my choice.

◆Current Status◆
> Elitia, Melissa, and Cion acquired Herculean Walnut Soufflé ⟶ Strength increased
> Arihito, Kyouka, Misaki, and Suzuna acquired Apple of Wit Pie ⟶ Maximum magic levels increased
> Theresia, Seraphina, and Madoka acquired Nimble Grape Syrup ⟶ Agility increased

Though my magic had been almost completely restored during dinner, when I checked it after my pie, it appeared to be half-empty. In other words, though my maximum magic power stores had increased, the magic itself had not, which made it seem like I'd used that much magic.

I never would've imagined it'd increase this much... This is basically two levels' worth, no?

"I feel so light... I have every faith that now I can block much more quickly, even while carrying a large shield."

"U-um, I also feel lighter...," Madoka added. "...Will this be of any help to you all?"

The ability to move faster was always a plus, no matter the situation. I had no doubt it would benefit Madoka, who would be joining us to steer the wagon.

"I hope these desserts were to your taste. Please do get in touch if you ever find yourselves in need of dishes cooked with special ingredients."

"Excuse me, Maria…might I speak with you for a moment?" Louisa called on her way out of the room. I hadn't the faintest idea what that was all about.

Part II: Scout

The taste of dessert lingering on our tongues, my friends and I left the Forest Diner. However, Louisa, Igarashi, Theresia, and I stayed back for a little while at a table on the first floor.

"Louisa, I've got to say…that was a pretty, you know, bold proposal."

"I do apologize. The thought came to me and I simply went with the impulse."

Louisa had called to Maria before she left and asked if the Chef would like to come to our lodgings after work later in the evening. The invitation had come as a complete surprise to me, but Maria looked at Louisa in silence for a few beats before matter-of-factly saying, "I still have to close up for the night. Would you mind if I came after?"

"Maria's been such a great help to us since we got to District Five," Igarashi commented. "Maybe it would be a good idea to use this opportunity to get to know each other a little better."

She had removed her armor before dinner and had now shed another layer, leaving only a knitted tunic very similar to the one she'd worn when we first came to the Labyrinth Country.

Why does all her clothing emphasize her curves so much?

"Mr. Atobe, how do you find her skills as a Chef?" Louisa asked.

"...Oh, I see what you're getting at."

"Huh? Wait, are you thinking about asking Maria to work for us exclusively, too?" Igarashi ventured, perfectly reading between the lines of what Louisa and I had said. All I could do in response to her astute observation was nod.

"Not only would this allow us to enjoy her delicious cooking more often, but I think it might be wise to have a specialist on hand who can make the best use of any valuable ingredients you acquire during seeking expeditions..."

"Yes, that's an excellent point," I agreed. "Thank you for taking the time to think about us, Louisa."

"I-it's nothing. Truth be told, a Receptionist like me should not involve herself in such matters..."

"Oh, hush. We all think of you as another party member. Go ahead and tell us anything that comes to mind. Maria will have the final say on this plan, of course."

"Kyouka..."

Igarashi and Louisa had become fast friends, partly, I assumed, because they were so close in age. They were sort of the designated "adult" members of the party. Seraphina would have normally been included in that category as well, but she had gone home ahead of us to train.

The Forest Diner wouldn't shut its doors for another two hours, but apparently some customers would stay past closing time until the early hours of the morning. Maria's shift ended whenever the customers at her assigned tables left, which this evening meant she would get out around eight-thirty.

"Thank you for waiting."

Changed out of her uniform, Maria carried a sack full of belongings over toward us. She wore a leather jacket and pants; topped off with that cap, her whole ensemble was very casual.

"Wow... Maria, you look like a different person from the Chef we know," Louisa marveled. "Do they even sell such stylish clothing in this country?"

"Yes, I purchased them in a store I dropped by when I was dispatched to District Six."

"I didn't know there was such good shopping there," said Igarashi. "I'd love to hear all about it."

"...I'll tell you about it later this evening, then."

Louisa and Igarashi exchanged gleeful looks. I thought it would be great if Maria joined our team, but more than that, I hoped she and the other ladies would get along.

Battling Hidden God parts provided invaluable experience for us. That said, those fights didn't help us rise in level. Our licenses would read we'd "defeated" an enemy, but those victories were evidently evaluated differently from those involving normal monsters.

We've filled in several experience bubbles... I guess it must be the rule here that Named Monsters are worth more experience points. If we take on another monster in our next seeking expedition, I'll bet a few of us should be able to level up. We'll probably run into a few battle opportunities when we go to the Tremulous Foothills to search for the Holy Stones, but should we try to avoid them and prioritize our resource search? It's a hard choice.

"...I once made my living as a Seeker...but my party hit a dead end in District Seven and disbanded shortly after," Maria explained. "Many of our members specialized in work better suited for supporting Seekers, though, so that may have played a part in our split."

"Yeah, I sooo get that. I'm a Gambler, so it's a struggle to find ways to help in battles. But my big bro Arihito always lets me pitch in."

"That's...that's just wonderful. We all start out as Seekers in this country, but whether we can successfully draw out our own strengths during battle relies on more than just suitability for the job. It depends on each person's sense, too."

Maria told us she often went out drinking with her coworkers after work, and just as often would have a drink at home by herself. After a little alcohol worked its way into her system, my overall impression of her changed. Her tongue loosened, and she spoke much more freely than while she was on the job. At this point, she had removed her leather jacket and cap and was chatting with us on the sofa, looking very at home. Misaki took it all in happily.

"…Mr. Atobe, the way Ms. Misaki refers to you—are you two perhaps related?" Maria asked.

"No, she just calls me that since I'm older than her…"

"You're *everybody's* brother, y'know," Misaki chimed in. "Although I think you miiight be a little more for Suzu or Ellie."

"It's not nice to talk about people behind their backs like that, Misaki," Igarashi warned. "Friendships can crack at the littlest things."

"Ah-ha…ha-ha… Let's pretend you didn't hear that. Say it's off the record."

"Hmm…? Off the record?" Maria asked.

"All right, how about you and I go take our baths, Misaki? Atobe has something important to discuss with Maria."

"Melissa and the others are prob there. You think Ferris hates water?"

I wonder. They say cats hate water, but Melissa's a great swimmer. Maybe Ferris doesn't mind it much, either.

Igarashi left the living room with Misaki in tow. Theresia stayed behind, waiting. I felt it would be too awkward to tell her she should go with them. I heard the group chatting boisterously as they headed to the baths. Maria, however, stayed where she was.

"Maria, what's your plan for the rest of the evening?"

"Louisa is sleeping off her drinks at the moment, so I think I'd like to take a bath with her later if I may. She asked if I would on the way here."

"Sounds good. So you may have already heard, but we were wondering..."

"If I could sign an exclusive contract with your party, correct? Yes, I am aware."

"Sorry to spring this on you so suddenly. We were actually still in District Seven, but we skipped a district to get here," I explained, figuring it probably would have been more appropriate to bring this sort of proposal up after we'd earned the right to officially seek in this district.

However, Maria shook her head lightly. "You and your party have already accomplished commendable feats in District Five. Also, I'm in a similar boat. By all rights, I should still be in District Seven, unable to move up in the ranks. But I transferred up here thanks to my skill as a Chef."

"You transferred...," I repeated. "I didn't know you could do that through the Guild."

"Yes. Such special exceptions can also be made for talented support staff. The Guild provides training to help us maintain our levels as well... I left District Seven as a level five, but have since grown to one level below the recommended level ten for this district."

A level-9 Chef—and one that surpasses my current level, at that. I wonder if the people you see around town in District Five are all at such high levels, too.

"When you and your party fought to quell the stampeding monsters here, you protected all sorts of people, from those who are too elderly to fight anymore to support staff who have for one reason or another gone down in level. Ever since I first heard about the amazing job you had done, I've been trying to think of how I could help you in return. I was already honored to have been able to serve you at the Forest Diner, so when you asked me to bake those desserts for you, I was overwhelmed with emotion."

"That's very kind of you... Actually, I should say the honor was all ours. My party and I have a pressing task to accomplish in District Five, so we wanted to come as quickly as we possibly could. We joined the effort to quell the stampede at the Guild's behest, a request that came with special permission to come to this district."

"...May I ask what that task is?"

"A rescue mission. We're trying to save someone important to one of our friends...which makes her important to us, too," I replied, giving Maria only the briefest bullet points. It didn't feel right to go into detail without Elitia's permission.

But would that be enough to earn Maria's trust? For a while she seemed to be deep in thought. Then, from her seat straight across from me, she looked me in the eye.

That's when I realized her eyes were not actually seeing me.

"...The reason I quit seeking was because a Named Monster stole almost all my vision from me. My party members said they would look for a way to get it back, but I told them not to. I didn't want to bind them in a search for that Named Monster."

"So does that mean...you supplement your vision with something else?"

"Yes. With my acute sense of smell from my line of work, and my hearing. These bracelets give me the Heightened Hearing 2 skill."

Maria removed one of the bracelets, gemstones tied together with a string, and handed it to me.

"Maria, is this...?"

"Would you please take one for me? I cannot assist you in battle. But I hope you will allow me to wait for your safe return here in town."

"...All right. I'll return this to you—I promise. I'll keep it on me until then."

"Of course. Expeditions in District Five come fraught with danger... I pray you will all return safely, despite the risks. I'd like to once more...no, once and many times over prepare meals to nourish you."

"Maria..."

"...This is what it means to invite a Chef to work exclusively with you. Do you understand?"

I had been thinking about hiring Maria to cater for us, about what we would need to provide and how we could compensate her. That was what I'd expected the negotiations for her exclusive contract would require. But our party and our supporters had never done anything like that before. Instead of writing up contracts, we'd talked things over and built our relationships on a foundation of caring.

"...I would love to entrust you with any rare ingredients we find in the dungeons and see what you could make with them—as long as you'll agree to join us at the table from time to time. Would that work for you? This is how we maintain our relationships with all our supporters."

"A Chef's place is in the kitchen. But that does sound very fun."

Maria extended her right hand. I shook it, after which she stood up and offered it again to Theresia.

"......"

"You always stay faithfully by Mr. Atobe's side, don't you? I was so pleased to see you enjoying your fill of my meals. I look forward to getting to know you better."

Though Theresia couldn't directly respond to Maria with words, her tail shook vigorously back and forth. It was just a feeling, but to me it seemed like she was saying, *Me too*.

As the baths in our apartment were occupied, I ambled over to the public baths right next door. With five silver coins, you could reserve a small, private bathing room. This establishment stayed open quite late into the night. The receptionist at the desk greeted me drowsily.

"So, that will be one...excuse me, two adults, counting your companion, correct?"

"Y-yes..."

Mixed bathing wasn't prohibited per se, but it still made me feel a little guilty.

"......"

Theresia pitter-pattered after me. No sooner had we entered

the dressing room and closed the door than she started reaching for the clasp to her suit.

"W-wait. Don't undress in front of me."

"……"

She obediently stopped what she was doing. Granted, I was struggling to get myself undressed, but this was no time to get cold feet. I stripped everything off in a flash, opened the door, and slipped into the bathing room. Right behind me, I heard the *snap* of the clasp unfastening.

"Arihito, are you taking Theresia with you again? Enjoy your bath."

"Arihito, my boy, I meant to provide you with my company in the bath this evening, but I had Ferris and Falma with me, you see. We supporting ladies need our own little spa day."

"Have a relaxing bath, Mr. Atobe. And do take care to wash Theresia's back for her."

Madoka, Ceres, and Falma had cheerfully sent us off. And yet, though we'd recently shared baths with groups of three or more, it had been quite a while since Theresia and I had taken a bath just the two of us. It brought back memories of when we'd first started out. Back then, I'd unintentionally gotten a glimpse of Theresia naked after she unexpectedly stripped before me, only for my younger companion to give me a few pats on the back. I still wasn't sure if that had been her way of reassuring me or what. Still, so much had changed since then, since we were two strangers who had just met.

Steam swirled around the room as the door slid open. Theresia stepped inside, naked except for the mask she couldn't remove.

"Here, Theresia. I'll start by washing your back."

"……"

"Hm? …You'd prefer I go first?"

Theresia nodded. I didn't mind if that's what she wanted, so I sat in the shower chair and turned my back to her.

"……"

"…Theresia?"

I didn't want to look behind me without good reason. But Theresia showed no signs of movement, so I grew worried and tried turning my head.

"……!"

"…S-sorry. I should've said something first."

She'd stopped me before I could look back, so I faced front once again.

Something's different; she's not always like this. And I know exactly when it started. Maybe the curse is changing something within her? Will the Evil Domination affect her more as it advances, or will nothing happen until its progress reaches 100?

"…Just a little longer. Just hold on a little longer, Theresia."

She started scrubbing. Her hands moved so gently, it almost broke my heart.

Part III: Revisiting Medium

After we returned to our suite, I was sitting in the living room when Suzuna, who'd apparently already taken her bath, came in. She closed the door behind her and sat across from me on the sofa.

"Arihito, there's a notification on my license."

```
◆Notification◆
> ARIADNE requested SUZUNA use MEDIUM
```

Ariadne had seemed somewhat reluctant to use Medium, but given she'd be able to read my thoughts if I tried to scrutinize why, I tried to keep my mind as clear as possible.

"...*You are overthinking things.*"

"*Sorry,*" I mentally replied. Suzuna also heard her, evidently, and grinned bashfully.

"All right, I'm going to let Ariadne into my body."

"Great, thanks."

Suzuna sat on the floor in a *seiza* position, closed her eyes, and began to concentrate. A faint blue light enveloped her frame, and a few locks of her flowing black hair floated gently.

"...Enter this vessel and let the world hear your voice..."

Suzuna intoned the incantation, at which her body suddenly listlessly slumped forward, and her hair took on the blue sheen of Ariadne's.

"It's been a while, Ariadne," I said.

"*To me, it does not feel as if much time has elapsed at all,*" the Hidden God replied in her usual detached way, though something about her overall presence felt different from the last time we'd communicated via Medium. "*The longer Seekers remain contracted to Hidden Gods, the more optimal their bonds become. Currently, I deem we still retain room for improvement.*"

She sounds mechanical, or like some super-advanced AI system— granted, Ariadne's not a robot, so that's just my random impression.

"*I am the product of my creator's invention. Therefore, your interpretation is partially valid.*"

"Sure, but we were all made by *something.*"

"*...There are vast differences between your physical and psycho-logical structures and my own. Nevertheless, while I remain present in this flesh, I can understand the physical aspects of human nature. As a result, I am capable of certain simulations.*"

"...Hm?"

I'd been pretty laid back, as we hadn't yet gotten down to business, but it sounded like Ariadne might've said something I shouldn't let slip by me.

"*It was a stroke of fortune to find Fylgja at this stage. Given her ability to instantaneously provide one party member with highly effective protection, she is one armament we cannot do without.*"

"Instantaneous high-powered protection... Can she also tele-port?"

Ariadne nodded, then stared at me intently. It seemed as if she wanted to say something. Suzuna's eyes glinted with Ariadne's characteristic gleam.

"…We can attempt a test now, but I will require a store of magical power before I am able to extract the full functions of my parts."

"So it's better not to use it here, then? All right, let's get started and give you some magic."

"Y-yes… Go ahead, Arihito," Suzuna said.

I wasn't sure if that meant she'd taken the reins again, or that Ariadne would temporarily hand them to her in moments like this.

Suzuna came over and sat by my side. After she turned her back to me, I placed my hand over her shoulder as I had before.

◆Current Status◆
> ARIHITO activated CHARGE ASSIST 1 —→ SUZUNA
  recovered magic
> SUZUNA activated ENERGY SYNC on ARIADNE's
  behalf
> ARIHITO's and SUZUNA's magic have achieved
  equilibrium

My Charge Assist provided the target with a little more magic than it cost me to activate. After I restored Suzuna's magic, our levels evened out with the help of Energy Sync to essentially create a machine in perpetual motion—a fancy way to say we could keep raising our devotion levels without expending any magic.

"So that's one round… All right, let's go one more— Ngh…"

"Suzuna, are you sure you don't want to take more of a break?"

"N-no, it's just… I'm fine. I'll get used to it soon enough."

I don't know if it's because she just got out of the bath, but

Suzuna feels a little warm—maybe I should touch her somewhere different each time so no one spot gets overheated.

"......"

I could feel Theresia's eyes boring a hole through me. Even though she knew what we were doing, it must've been a bizarre sight.

"There is a limit to how much you can raise devotion levels in one session. That maximum depends on factors such as the involved parties' levels and the time elapsed since the previous session, but we yet have room to grow. Continue until I instruct otherwise."

Until she instructs us otherwise—how many times will that be? I'm just gonna have to keep a totally clear head to get through this.

"Okay," I said to Suzuna, "let's do one more round…!"

"Go ahead…!"

The magic flowing within me streamed through my palm and into Suzuna. All the excess magic from Charge Assist that Suzuna's body couldn't contain floated off her like glittering grains of light.

I see. That's how Ariadne's magic gets charged.

Two times, then three—the more magic I poured into Suzuna, the more her shoulders relaxed. Maybe she had gotten used to it, just as she'd said. Four times, five times; I'd moved my hand around between rounds, but now I was running out of space.

"You're getting pretty feverish… Want to take a break?"

"…Arihito… I'm all right. Please continue… Next time, go a little lower…"

A little lower put me right above the small of her back. Not wanting to go too far, I made sure to stay squarely within what counted as her mid-back—until Suzuna reached behind her and grabbed my wrist.

"A little...lower. It'll make the magic circulation more efficient."

"O-okay... Let's do this. *Charge Assist.*"

"...!"

She claimed my hand placement affected the efficacy of the transmission, but I wondered how much. That said, I did feel my magic streaming faster into Suzuna than when I'd had my hand higher up on her back.

"*...Continue exactly as you are. I should be able to suppress the mental shock waves...the fluctuations...for three more rounds.*"

"Y-you got it... Just three more, then."

"All right, that's...doable... I should be...okay..."

Suzuna looked anything but okay, but I felt too awkward to bring it up. As far as I knew, though, this process shouldn't hurt her. I kept activating Charge Assist, my hand right where Ariadne had told me to leave it, sliding only a little from the middle to either side. I wondered if there was some reason the small of her back worked well for this.

"*...Every human frame has a corporeal celestial map delineating each magic receptor and connecting them together. Ideally, one should cycle through every receptor in order, instead of simply sending magic into the body,*" Ariadne explained, then turned around to face me as if to signal our time was up. I never could've predicted what she said next:

"*In fact, most of these receptors are located on the front of the body.*"

"...On the front?"

"*Because your skills work only on those in front of you, you cannot use these front-facing points. However, those same skills should allow you to reach around from behind the back to touch these nodes.*"

"Y-yeah... We can't do that, Ariadne."

Even laying my hands on Suzuna's back felt a little improper, so reaching around in front was completely out of the question. Would Ariadne understand? She'd averted her eyes, but now she glanced over at me.

"*...I see no issue, either morally or in terms of your relationship—* No, I can't do it! I can't make Arihito do that...!" Suzuna cut in halfway.

She must've gotten pretty flustered, because she crawled backward and accidentally pushed me down on the sofa.

"S-sorry, I...!"

"I-it's fine, no need to apologize..."

"*I have caused a misunderstanding. I should not have spoken for the Shrine Maiden without first asking her consent. I will endeavor to ensure this does not happen again...*"

Ariadne spoke for one brief beat as Suzuna pushed herself up, but then Suzuna took over once more. She seemed to feel really guilty, and honestly, I did, too. What was I supposed to do in moments like these...?

"......"

Theresia scooted into my line of sight and held a hand down on her lizard mask. Was she trying to say what I thought she was? That plan could possibly only further anger Suzuna, but I just had to go for it.

"...Suzuna, I'm the one who should apologize."

"...Ah..."

I patted Suzuna's head. Only after I felt her silky hair did I realize one crucial thing.

"S-sorry—you probably don't want people touching your hair after you just washed it..."

"...No, it's fine. It's all dry by now."

"...Right."

A peek at Suzuna's face was all I needed to decide whether to continue. She looked a little embarrassed, but she stood stock-still with my hand on her head.

"Thank you. This feels very calming..."

"...Has Ariadne left? Because your hair..."

"Oh...y-yes, it seems so. She's a little mischievous, isn't she?" Suzuna noted, although she didn't ask what Ariadne had communicated to me telepathically. Our devotion levels had evidently satisfactorily risen—along with Ariadne's magic.

"...Eep?!"

"Wh-what's wrong?"

Suddenly, Suzuna yelped. I whipped around to see why, only to notice Misaki had at some point sneaked into the room.

"Th-the thing is...you see, I was wondering how Suzuna was

doing and came to check, but the vibe in here felt kinda off, and it seemed like some super-serious stuff was going on... S-sorryyy!"

"Hey—! Misaki, don't just run away...!"

"Calm down, Misaki... Ahhh...?!"

Misaki flung the door open to find Igarashi, Louisa, and Falma on the other side.

"Oh my," said Louisa. "I'd thought perhaps we could all enjoy a bit of fun as we would on a little adventure, but..."

"I do apologize," Falma added, "but it was past the time we had expected Suzuna to return, and we were debating whether to come in and call her..."

"Sorry, I thought we should've been a little quieter...," said Igarashi.

"No, I'm sorry for keeping her for so long..."

"Thank you. We're all done now. Well then, Arihito, I'll head back to my room."

Suzuna got her things and went back to the bedrooms with the rest of the ladies—or so I thought, until the door opened once more and Falma popped her head inside.

"...Mr. Atobe, have you been naughty?"

"N-no. I promise I didn't do anything."

"Hee-hee... Considering what Misaki said, then... Oops, I think perhaps I'm teasing you."

"Falma, what—?"

"Good night, Mr. Atobe."

Before I could ask what she meant, Falma's smiling face disappeared behind the door.

"......"

"...What's up?"

Theresia had made to touch my shoulder, but when I turned around she snapped her hand back.

"Guess we should get to bed... You should get a good night's rest, too, Theresia."

"......"

She nodded and curled up on the sofa. I brought her a blanket and laid it over her so she wouldn't catch a cold. Theresia drew it in close, only her head peeping out, and looked at me.

I didn't check the curse mark on her nape. Evidently, the Evil Domination had not progressed much since we'd last left the labyrinth. I followed suit and lay down, then closed my eyes. Just as I was wondering whether I'd be able to get some sleep, I heard Ariadne's voice.

"...*My dear devotee, may you rest soundly in my protection.*"

It echoed like a lullaby in my mind. Rest when you must; that was the quickest route to reaching our goal. I cracked my eyes open one last time and saw Theresia still facing me, already fast asleep.

Part IV: Unlocking

The next morning, Maria ordered supplies from the Forest Diner and prepared breakfast for us. She'd apparently stayed up talking for a bit with Louisa and the others the previous night, but she was still the first to emerge from their bedroom ready for the day. By the time she entered the living room, she'd already donned her apron, now over casual clothes instead of her uniform.

"Good morning, Mr. Atobe. Would you like bread with your breakfast? I've also cooked some rice if that's what you prefer."

"Sure, I'll have rice, please... Ah, uhhh, sorry. You just woke up and I'm already putting you to work."

"...On the contrary. Thank you for allowing me to stay the night. I hadn't planned on it, but it made me very happy to hear you welcome me so warmly."

"I'm glad to hear it. Are the others still asleep?"

"Ms. Kyouka and Louisa are awake. I also saw Ms. Suzuna in the bathroom."

Evidently, the adult faction of our group rose early to prepare for the day, while I was still rubbing the sleep from my eyes.

I should learn to be more like them.

"......"

Theresia also had already woken, her blanket folded neatly on the sofa. She toddled over to me and folded my coverlet, too.

"Thank you. Did you sleep well last night?"

"......"

She nodded. I didn't want to seem overly worried; she looked fine, so I figured I could rest easy for now.

Melissa and her family were staying in another room we'd been able to rent. After deciding I'd go over and ask them to join us for breakfast, I started changing into my usual suit.

Before returning to her party's home base, Ferris told us she would stay in District Five for the foreseeable future and once again promised to help with our mission—or at least that's how Melissa interpreted her mother's thoughts for us. We were just about to head out for the day, but not before a chat with Melissa. I'd told the others, who had already stepped out, that we'd catch up after.

"My mom's twice as strong as I am. She'll be a big help. She used to be a Ranger, but now she's a Felid Fighter."

"Ranger... Is that similar to a member of a specialized military force?"

"She said before she came to this country, she was a...parole officer?"

She must've been much more active than I'd been as a regular office worker. And yet even she had experienced the cold grip of death. That was what it meant to be a demi-human. I wanted to learn how to turn Theresia back into a human, a technique Ferris and I both longed to discover. But helping us with our battle against the Simian Lord would eat up the time she would otherwise be spending on that.

"I...don't understand everything my mom is thinking. But if I go, she'll fight with me... That's what it seemed like she was saying."

"...I see. We'll have to find a way to thank her, for sure."

"I think she'd say she doesn't need thanks. She was always the driving force pulling my dad everywhere. She's pretty open and frank." Melissa's gaze softened with fond recollection, though it was also undeniably tinted with sadness. "My dad wouldn't stop talking about you last night. He said you're amazing."

"O-oh yeah…?"

The compliment left me a little embarrassed, but once I realized that meant he trusted me, I felt a sense of relief. Rikerton was lending us the assistance of his entire family, after all.

"My mom kept nodding along… But then I felt like a third wheel, so I asked Suzuna and Misaki to go outside with me."

"You did, huh…? W-well, that's, uh…"

I stayed cool as she related the story, but Melissa was essentially telling me she'd given her parents some private time, right? Her consideration impressed me, but I wasn't sure how to handle this extremely delicate topic.

"…By the time I got back, they were both asleep. It looked like my mom had put my dad to sleep."

Why is she telling me all this? Maybe she wants to keep me up to date with whatever she does when she's away from the party, even if it's with family? I appreciate that.

"Did you share the bed with them, too?"

"…My mom said it was okay."

"Right… That's good. It feels nice, doesn't it?"

I didn't grow up with my parents, but sometimes the teachers at the orphanage would take naps with us, and it was incredible how much it put me at ease. Melissa was mature and a formidable fighter, but she still had some childish aspects that were more in line with her age. As the adult in the situation, I knew I'd need to keep watching over her. Although I can't say that sharing the same bed is how we should all be going about that.

"…!"

I patted Melissa's head, which startled her at first. But then she lowered her eyes just a little.

"…I'm not a kid…but…"

I'd thought she might protest along those lines. But before I pulled my hand back, I heard her whisper:

"…I guess…I don't mind so much…if you do it, Arihito…"

"A-all right…"

Although I was relieved that she wasn't angry, I wasn't sure whether I should continue since Melissa was acting so different from normal.

"…Suzuna said you patted her head, too. Misaki said her heart pounded just watching."

Yeah, I guess they would share that info among themselves. I wonder what they think of me, the constant head petter… Just imagining it gives me the creeps.

"But…that wasn't all they said…"

"Hm…? Wh-what wasn't?"

"…Never mind. I don't want you to change."

"Huh…?"

"I'm gonna go."

With that brief goodbye, Melissa left. In any event, it seemed the head pets hadn't been a fiasco. Not that I should break them out every day, but…

It sounded like she was trying to say something... Maybe she
wanted me to activate Charge Assist? Magic should be replenished
with a good night's sleep, but maybe there's some kind of mood
aspect to it, too?

"......"

As I got lost in my thoughts, the door opened and Theresia
peeked in at me. She'd apparently been loyally waiting for me outside. I double-checked that I hadn't forgotten anything and then
rushed out into the hall.

We first asked Falma to continue where we'd left off the day before
and open the remaining Black Box. We couldn't dismiss the chance
that we might face off against another armament, so I had everyone gather and prepare for battle.

After teleporting to the chest cracking room, Falma held her
hand over the Black Box. A half-translucent, three-dimensional
maze unfolded from within. Falma guided her magic through it.

"Ohhh... So we're going easy on me today, are we...? But I
know the truth. There's always a catch... Heh-heh, see? What did
I tell you? There's no point in trying to fool me, my dear... I see
right through you... Not there, here...!"

She must have been getting used to opening these Black Boxes;
usually, our palms would get sweaty with anticipation as we
watched her fiercely tackle the mazes, but this one took hardly any
time at all.

"It's opening…!"

Lines etched into the surfaces of the black cube glowed with a faint blue light, which then expanded and blinded us with a sheet of white.

```
◆Chest Opened◆
Black Box: Acquired in ?Treasure Labyrinth
> ?Magic tool
> ?Rusty weapon
> ?Plate mail
> ?Charm
> ?Cloak
> Mystrium Medallion
> Gold coins x832
> Silver coins x158
> Copper coins x153
> White olden kingdom coins x18
```

There were also a few more items not listed, but they were either damaged or things we could easily buy, so I decided to ignore them for now.

"So many coins, just like always…and that's awesome and all, but what the heck is this…?"

"Misaki, you'd better not touch that just yet," Elitia warned.

Misaki chuckled bashfully. Misaki—not to mention the rest of us—already had a few chilling experiences with unexpected teleportation, like when she'd found the platform leading to a hidden floor in the Field of Dawn.

"Is this...a magical tool? It looks like I can use Appraise 2 on it."

"All right," I said. "Be careful, Madoka."

"Okay, I'll try my best!"

Using her magnifying lens and being careful not to touch anything, Madoka closely inspected what looked like a metal utensil. What exactly was it? I couldn't even begin to imagine just by looking at it. That said, its frame did look somewhat similar to an umbrella.

"...I...I got it...!"

◆★Magical Bonnet Canopy◆
> Produces a magic-powered bonnet canopy. Durability depends on the party's level.
> Increases interior storage capacity.
> If destroyed and reverted to normal capacity, any overflow items will be ejected.
> Once destroyed, 180 seconds must pass before the bonnet canopy can be redeployed.

"A bonnet canopy... Like the kinds on covered prairie wagons?" I asked.

"If so, would that mean we could set up a tent wherever we like?" wondered Igarashi.

She was probably right, but Seraphina seemed to have another idea.

"I believe I've thought of another use for it. If we affix it to the top of the wagon and deploy it, then…"

"The wagon's storage capacity would increase… Plus, the canopy itself would provide some protection…!"

If used efficiently, the canopy could help those of our members who needed to ride on the wagon. And as long as we kept a close eye on its condition, we could probably use it as a tent for camping out in labyrinths, too.

"Let's get this attached to our wagon," I told the group. "Thank you, Falma. You've helped us uncover another helpful treasure."

"My pleasure. Ever since you've permitted me to purchase your extra armaments, my shop has gained quite the favorable reputation in District Eight… I do, however, ask the Guild to sell them for me to ensure they reach a wide audience."

Falma risked drawing too much attention to her shop if she sold everything on her own, since all the weapons we wound up not needing were far stronger than the equipment available to newcomers in the district.

"As for the rusty weapon and plate mail…," Madoka began. "I'm sorry—it looks like we'll need to use a High-Grade Appraisal Scroll. That, or I'd need to acquire Appraise 3."

"High-grade, huh…? I guess we can't just sand away the rust to find out what these items are," I said.

"That leaves this protective charm and cloak," added Suzuna. "The one that looks like a cape."

Moving on, Madoka appraised the two items Suzuna had

mentioned. We could always use more charms—this one most was likely a type of ankh, given its shape—since we benefited simply by having them on hand.

◆★Guardian Angel Ankh◆
> Slightly augments defense from physical attacks
> Slightly augments defense from magical attacks
> Nullifies certain status ailments with a set probability
> Reduces power behind enemy breath-type attribute attacks
> Can at times restore nearby party members' stamina corresponding to damage taken from enemy

◆★Dhampir Cape◆
> Augments defense from physical attacks
> Provides Metal Resistance 1
> Provides Charm Resistance 2
> Can inflict Impulsive status on enemy
> Inflicts Craving status on women who lose vitality with it equipped
> Possesses a hidden power

That Guardian Angel Ankh should go to one of our defensive frontliners, either Seraphina or Cion. Is it called a Dhampir Cape because it's black? Given how devastating the Passion status ail-ment is, this Craving status must be really dangerous. I wonder why it doesn't affect men?

"Dhampir... Those are half-vampire/half-humans, right?" Misaki asked. "I mean, if vampires even exist in the Labyrinth Country..."

"Would that then mean that this Craving status makes you want to drink blood?" Igarashi wondered aloud.

"Either way, it can't be good," said Elitia. "We could look into it more at the Archive, but I think it's best if Arihito takes it since he won't be at risk of getting this status."

"Ooh, I bet Ari-poo looks *amaaazing* in a cape. Especially since he totally had that dark, shadowy vibe going for him at the beginning."

I probably just looked like a haggard corporate grunt..., I thought, but I tried the cape on anyway. I planned to take it off immediately if that hidden power felt unsafe, but nothing really came up. It was actually surprisingly comfortable, lighter and more breathable than it looked.

"...Hard to know what to say when it fits him so perfectly, isn't it?" Igarashi admitted.

"Forget half-bloodsucker/half-human, though—he looks *exactly* like one of those monster hunters! Don't ya think?"

"It looks lovely on you, Arihito," Suzuna told me.

"I-in any case...I think either Seraphina or Cion should use this ankh, since they need to protect us more often."

After everyone agreed, I decided the Guardian Angel Ankh

would go to Seraphina, who at times had to cover us all from our enemies' most powerful attacks.

"Then all we've got left is... Doesn't this look kinda like the thingamabob Commander Dylan gave us?"

"A Mystrium Medallion... Those are more valuable than a Magistite Medallion," Seraphina noted.

Meaning those Seekers who'd achieved such great heights fell before Alphecca. I don't know how this medallion came to be locked away in this Black Box, but we should try to return it to its rightful owner. Even if that's not possible, we have to handle it with proper respect.

Our chest cracking done, we set off for another labyrinth expedition in search of Holy Stones. Falma and Madoka stayed behind, taking care of all the items we'd acquired from the box.

"I'll switch places with Melissa and stay in town today," Madoka said. "Please be very careful, Arihito—and the rest of you..."

"Don't worry, we'll be back—I promise. Thank you so much again, Falma."

"I should be thanking you. I look forward to hearing all about your further exploits this evening."

With that, we left the special chest cracking room. A thin curtain of clouds had covered the skies before we went in. Now, however, we could see the brilliant sun peeking through pockets in the veil.

CHAPTER 2

Curse-Lifting Ore and an Encounter with a Formidable Foe

Part I: The Tremulous Foothills, Floor One

The Tremulous Foothills were said to be located in a slightly elevated area of District Five's northern sections. On our way there, we came across another party apparently headed for a different labyrinth.

"...Natalia, aren't they...?"

"I knew we would meet again."

Among their members were Natalia and Leonard, two Seekers we'd found on the second floor of the Twilight Lakeside Stroll. They'd been under attack by the Cursed Water Serpent Worshipper when we jumped in to their rescue. Leonard was skilled in a martial art that revolved around kicks. Now, however, his legs were equipped with something like greaves. Maybe the labyrinth they were headed to didn't have very sandy terrain. Natalia was wearing a fluffy fur hat that made her look like a hunter from some snowy arctic land.

Their party was called Eisenritter, if I remembered correctly, and today they had two more women with them. One had a wild, pirate-inspired look with a bandanna tied around her head, and the other wore glasses, a cap, and some sort of tactical vest.

"Ah...i-is that my harpoon? The one I dropped...?"

"I found it on the first floor of the Twilight Lakeside Stroll and picked it up for you. I'm sorry; I forgot to return it."

Evidently, the trident Nelzex Harpoon Igarashi carried belonged to the woman in the bandanna. Though tough and intense in appearance, she broke into a friendly smile as soon as she retrieved the weapon from Igarashi.

"I can't believe how spineless I was, but that ghost or whatever hit us with a sneak attack and we got separated from the hired sword in our party. I couldn't get any closer to the Water Serpent, and arrows were flying at us, though I couldn't tell from where... I really did Natalia and Leonard dirty. I'm supposed to be the front-line tank, but I couldn't protect them."

"We should've had a plan for safely getting out of those phantom-infested shores. Also, sell-swords really won't do more than they're paid for, so we shouldn't have brought one with us on such a challenging expedition... You have it nice, little fella, with so many people in your party."

"Natalia," I said, "I'm not so sold on that *little fella*... I'm twenty-nine, you know."

"Heh-heh... We can't help but see you as a little guy, though, more than an older gent."

Not once had I ever been told I looked younger than my age.

But perhaps this had something to do with Natalia's culture in her home country, so I let it slide.

"E-excuse me... Please allow me to thank you for saving my friends the other day. My name is Yuuho Nanamori, the healer of this party."

"My name is Arihito Atobe."

"Ah, so you *are* from Japan. My name in kanji means 'having a long walk in seven forests,'" the woman in the tactical vest explained as she readjusted her glasses. I got the impression that her Japanese name had something to do with shogi.

"...S-sorry," she said, "you didn't even ask and yet here I am, babbling..."

"O-oh, no, not at all. The kanji in my name means 'having a person in the back section.'"

"Ah, so we share a kanji between us. I didn't expect to have something like that in common."

"Atobe and his friends saved us, Yuuho," said the bandanna woman. "There's nothing wrong with small talk, but we should do something to thank them, too."

I hadn't even considered asking them for compensation, but maybe they had some information we could use. My party seemed content to leave the talking to me.

"My name's Vanessa. I'm the eldest in our party, but that puts me at three years younger than you, Atobe. As you can see, I'm a Fisher."

I shook Vanessa's outstretched hand. She reminded me of the

Four Seasons ladies. Somehow, I got the feeling she and Ryouko would get along.

"About how many labyrinths have you explored in this district?" I asked them.

"We've checked out eight of them, just barely scratching the surface of the first floor, though. I wanted to go after the Water Serpent with this harpoon, since it seemed like it'd be useful, but it wasn't that easy."

"I imagine it must've been a tough experience, but I'm glad you're all right," I replied. "We're about to raid the Trembling Foothills ourselves..."

"If you're looking for ore and the like, watch out for the monsters lurking in those areas. Some camouflage as rocks so well, you don't even realize they're there until they move."

"Thank you, Leonard. I'll keep that in mind, man."

That seemed to surprise Leonard for a second, but he quickly smiled and held out his right hand, which I shook as I had Vanessa's.

"Anything else you care to know, little fella?"

"Mr. Atobe, if I may?"

"Yes, of course, Seraphina."

"Would any of you happen to know where we can locate what's known as a Holy Stone?"

"Looks like you really need Lady Luck on your side if you want to find those rare metals. We're keepin' our eyes out for Holy Stones, too, but unfortunately haven't spotted any yet," Vanessa explained.

"Weapons fortified with a Holy Stone would've probably come in handy against those phantoms. But not everything falls into your lap as you like, I suppose," said Leonard, his eyes cast down toward his greaves.

He had a point. Holy-attribute weapons would've probably been useful in a battle against the Ice Remnant ghost monsters.

"Wait a moment—Arihito, did you just call Lena by—?"

"I've heard you can find the Holy Stones on the first floor, too. They apparently glow in dark places, so keep an eye out for that. If you'll excuse us..."

Cutting Yuuho off before she could finish her sentence, Leonard gave us the extra tip and walked away.

"Oh, I know," said Yuuho. "If you're going to be excavating, I've got something that might help. It's called a Dwarf's Mattock."

"A mattock... You mean a pickax?"

"Yes, ones used in mining ore. It's a magical tool, so it may look small, but it cuts into the dirt like butter. Please feel free to take my spare, if you'd like."

Yuuho rummaged unsuccessfully through the countless pockets of her tactical vest until she finally found the mattock and handed it to me. Then, with a light wave, she ran off to catch up with her party members.

"Connections are vital, aren't they...? I cannot help but be convinced of it now," Seraphina noted.

"Indeed. We just need to find that Holy Stone."

I tucked the mattock away in my bag. Seeing as we were heading for foothills, I wondered if we should've prepared more for a proper hike. But neither Leonard nor his friends had mentioned anything, so chances were we'd be okay without special preparations.

"If this rests on luck, then I guess you're up, Misaki," Elitia mused.

"Luck's the only thing keepin' me alive, anyway. By the way, Ari-poo, remember how I've got my Bat Leather Cape? Now we're all matchy-matchy. Kinda like a couple's outfit."

"That's not quite right… But at least you look happy, Misaki."

"You gotta find happiness in the little things, right?"

What mattered most was my equipment's utility, although the idea of a couple's outfit left me a little unsettled…but I put that out of my mind for the moment.

"I'll bet your Big Lotto will be a big help here, Misaki," I said.

"Yep, yep, absoluuutely. One round of that and it'll be *tsumo* for me!"

"…*Tsumo?*"

Clearly, Misaki had played her fair share of mahjong. Melissa was apparently unfamiliar, so Misaki explained it referred to the moment when you draw your own winning tile in the game. The mention warmed a little nostalgic corner of my heart.

As we kept on walking, the ground rose into a gentle, spiraling slope. At the top, we came upon a large, ringlike structure of stacked stones. Through the ring we saw not a continuation of the outside scene but a view of what looked like the inside of a labyrinth. Seraphina dipped in first, and the rest of us followed her in formation. The sense of teleporting hit me as I felt the air around me change. It felt more elevated than the town's, but not at all thin—only a little cool.

We then found ourselves on a rocky stretch of land underneath a big, blue sky. A game trail led up to the summit of the mountain, whose face was covered with towering boulders we had to crane our necks to see. They formed formidable obstacles blocking the way, but the tracks Seekers before us had left cutting around them had naturally created a path through.

"This totally takes me back to when we went hiking in, like, middle school. All we need is some gym jerseys and backpacks and we've got a perfect reenactment going on."

"This mountain is so big... Getting back down will be a real challenge."

"Watch where you're walking, everyone," I cautioned. "You too, Cion."

"Bow!"

But Cion hardly needed my warning. Apparently cut out for this type of terrain, she trotted along without any trouble. What impressed me more was Seraphina, who carried her enormous shield yet showed no signs it hindered her at all.

"I don't see any monsters, but it looks like there's a bird over there," Elitia noted, pointing out a ptarmigan-type bird the likes of which I'd only ever seen on TV. It looked a little small for a monster, though, and my license didn't recognize it as a threat, either.

"Think we could just scratch up that boulder over there and get our metals?" asked Misaki.

"I wonder. If metal was what we were after, we could try using the mattock, but...I doubt we'd find any Holy Stones around here," I told her.

"If they were here, these stones would all be broken up by now."

Hiking took a bit of effort, so from then on we abandoned our chat and focused on the climb.

After about an hour, we came to a fork with one path leading farther up the mountain and another tracing along a ridge. We found the remains of a campsite beneath the roof of a nearby boulder. It must have come under attack, though, because the tent had been torn up and abandoned, and traces of blood still stained the rock face.

"If we take too long here, we'll have to camp out, too...," Elitia noted. "In an uncomfortably dangerous place, at that."

"Look, there's a hole blasted into the rock itself... I guess there's a monster out here that can do that," Igarashi added.

As the two inspected the roughed-up campsite, I used Hawk Eyes to survey the area—and landed on movement. Some sort of rabbit had come out from behind a big boulder along the ridge. Its fur was light pink, and it at least looked pretty adorable. And yet my mind raced back to the first monster I'd encountered in the Labyrinth Country: that white, fluffy Cotton Ball that had so suddenly and viciously attacked us.

"Hey, guys, check that out. I think it's a monster. What should we do?"

"It looks…like a Cotton Ball. But we can't let our guard down. It is a District Five monster, after all."

"…Grrrr…"

Cion's hackles were clearly raised. Still, it didn't *look* very dangerous from here.

```
◆Monster Encountered◆
> ?Peach-Pink Monster
Level Unknown
On Guard
Resistance Unknown
Dropped Loot: ???
```

"Some help this thing is, huh…?"

"We don't want it following after us if we take the path up the mountain, so I think we'd better fight here where we have space," Elitia reasoned.

"Good point… All right. Let me shoot at it first and see how it goes."

Since I wasn't sure of its resistance, I debated whether to try and give it a weakness with Force Shot: Freeze or go for a status ailment. With no guarantee either would work, I decided to go for the one that'd have the biggest impact: the status ailment.

"Arihito, I'll take aim as well," said Suzuna.

"Thanks. Stagger your shot, about a second after mine…!"

"Okay…!"

```
◆Current Status◆
> ARIHITO activated VINE SHOT
> SUZUNA activated FORBIDDEN ARROW
```

My slingshot's vine bullet and Suzuna's arrow flew toward the target.

I was afraid of that…!

"SHAHGIIII!!"

Out of what looked like nothing but a pink fluff ball sprouted two gigantic arms that then wrapped themselves around the monster's body, the picture of an impregnable defensive stance.

```
◆Current Status◆
> ?PEACH-PINK MONSTER activated BOXER'S FISTS →
  Unfolded arms
> ?PEACH-PINK MONSTER activated PEEK-A-BOO STYLE
  → Defense increased
Nullified VINE SHOT
```

My bullet bounced off the monster, and its defensive stance remained strong. Still, I added my support to Suzuna's staggered shot in an attempt to find even the smallest opening.

```
◆Current Status◆
> ARIHITO activated ATTACK SUPPORT 2 → Support
  Type: FORCE SHOT: FREEZE
> FORBIDDEN ARROW hit ?PEACH-PINK MONSTER
?PEACH-PINK MONSTER was Frozen
```

"GEEEE...GEESHAAA!!"

"A-a little tyke would *never* screech like that...!!"

The monster froze for a moment, then immediately snapped out of it—almost as if it was merely stunned. Even so, the Forbidden Arrow did seem to hit the beast, which looked as if it cringed in pain for a split second.

"Now...!"

Elitia was already on the move. She'd activated Comet Raid and was closing in on the monster, though eschewing the most direct route for one filled with twists and turns—she knew exactly how dangerous those arms could be if they got to her up close. Igarashi and Theresia also charged from the opposite flank, while Melissa rode Cion hot on Elitia's heels, aiming for an opening after her attack.

"*Warning. The next attack will cause devastating damage to my devotees—*" I heard Ariadne say. It was all I needed to grasp the impending danger. Our enemy was preparing a big move aimed at those in the rear: Suzuna, Misaki, and me.

For the first time in a while, I felt the chill of death.

I can't let this be the end. How could it happen so suddenly, so quickly, and now of all times—?

"SHAHGYAAAAAA!!"

◆Current Status◆
> ?Peach-Pink Monster was revealed to be ★Roving Tempest Demon Rabbit
> ★Roving Tempest Demon Rabbit activated Cannon Form → Arms transformed
> ★Roving Tempest Demon Rabbit activated Rabbit Tornado

The pink monster's arms coalesced to form one huge cannon-like structure. It charged for a second, waited leisurely until Elitia's and the others' attacks reached it, then unleashed a pink storm over a ridiculously wide range. Neither Suzuna nor Misaki could so much as move—and neither could I. But Seraphina did not run. She stood before us and raised her shield, no doubt fully aware that if the blow hit her, it would take her life.

Defense Support isn't going to cut it—1 or 2. But there is one move that could give us a chance. That's exactly why she's planted herself in front of us.

Fylgja, please... Protect Seraphina...!

Seraphina began to shine brightly, with a brilliance that seemed to struggle directly against the tempest portending destruction to all before it. And then—

"My name is Fylgja, she who arms her Hidden God and protects her devotees."

"Haaaaah...!!"

Seraphina let out a roar as she activated every defensive skill in her power. All sound drained from the world as Suzuna, Misaki, and I stood there, unable to do anything but watch.

Part II: The Labyrinth-Wise

"...!!"

The Rabbit Tornado tore into the rocky terrain as it barreled into Seraphina, whose armor had transformed. Ariadne had summoned Fylgja, and her protection.

◆Current Status◆
> Arihito requested temporary assistance from Ariadne
> Ariadne summoned Fylgja
> Fylgja activated Change Armor ⟶ Fortified Seraphina's Guardian's Mail +4
> Seraphina activated Aura Shield and Defense Force
> Fylgja activated Construct ⟶ Defenses will be fortified with every activation of a defensive skill

"Khh...urggh...!!"

Seraphina struggled against the tempest for a second that seemed to stretch on forever. My defensive powers might not make the slightest difference. But I didn't care—as long as I could support her in the slightest way.

"Seraphina, I'll support you!"

◆Current Status◆
> Arihito activated Defense Support 2 ⟶ Support Type: Guard Arm
> Rabbit Tornado hit Seraphina
Arihito's resistance reduced damage

My armor's shining...and so is my Dhampir's Cape. Oh, I see... Ariadne's Guard Arm and all the resistances I have get applied to Seraphina through Defense Support 2...!

"Aaaaaah…!!"

""Eeeek…!""

◆Current Status◆
> Seraphina's ★Mirrored Shell Pavis +1 repelled
  Rabbit Tornado
> ★Roving Tempest Demon Rabbit activated Arm Form
  and Whirlwind Fists ⟶ Nullified Rabbit Tornado
> ★Mirrored Shell Pavis +1's durability
  decreased
> Fylgja was unequipped
> ★Roving Tempest Demon Rabbit began charging
  breath attack

Seraphina rebuffed the Rabbit Tornado, sending it barreling back. Even so, the gusts swept Misaki and Suzuna off their feet. I only just barely caught them from behind.

That skill activation consumed more magic than expected. I must carefully consider when to provide support.

"Lady Fylgja, you have my gratitude…!" Seraphina called.

Luckily, we'd managed to fend off this one attack, but an instantaneous, high-powered defense came at a heavy cost. The brilliance peeled off Seraphina's armor, which then resumed its normal shape. Her Mirrored Shell Pavis could potentially reflect a breath attack to its instigator. It activated this power, bouncing Rabbit Tornado back, but the Demon Rabbit rapidly spun its arms to create a gale that canceled out the rebounded storm. Rabbit Tornado was a breath-type attack, which evidently meant the Demon Rabbit would need to recharge before unleashing it again.

"Keep your eyes on me!" Elitia yelled at her foe.

"SHWOOO...!"

◆Current Status◆
> ELITIA activated COMET RAID ⟶ Added SWORD BARRIER
> ★ROVING TEMPEST DEMON RABBIT attacked ⟶ ELITIA evaded

Elitia seized the opening, drawing the Demon Rabbit's attention to her and ducking under the arms it whipped out at her as she picked up speed, running so low to the ground, she was almost crawling.

"Flicker in brilliance and scatter...!"

"SHAHGIIII!"

"Elitia, I'll support you!"

Right now, we need to focus on the number of hits—as long as we make contact, we can absolutely chip away at it with the set damage from Attack Support 1.

◆Current Status◆
> ARIHITO activated ATTACK SUPPORT 1
> ELITIA activated ULTIMATUM ⟶ Attack power and speed increased
Added SCARLET TRAILS
> ★ROVING TEMPEST DEMON RABBIT activated SHIELD FORM

> ELITIA activated STAR PARADE ⟶ Number of
  attacks increased
> ELITIA activated LUMINOUS FLOW
> ★ROVING TEMPEST DEMON RABBIT activated MACHINE GUN
  BLOCK

"SHARARARARARA!!"

With terrifying speed, the Demon Rabbit transformed its arms into a shield and blocked all of Elitia's attacks. All we needed was a hit for the support damage to kick in, but we couldn't even get one to count.

"RARARARARAH!!"

"…!"

"Ellie!"

◆Current Status◆
> KYOUKA activated THUNDERBOLT ⟶ Hit ★ROVING
  TEMPEST DEMON RABBIT
★ROVING TEMPEST DEMON RABBIT was Electrocuted
13 support damage

At the rate things were going, every single one of Elitia's blows would be rebuffed, and she'd be left vulnerable to attack. Luckily, Igarashi jumped in at the very last second with a magical attack to back her up.

"Haaah!"

"SHAHGIIII…!!"

"GYAGYA...!"

The Demon Rabbit failed to thwart Elitia's strikes, which drew erupting pink sprays from all over the monster's body. Melissa and Cion then closed in on the enemy, showering it with a stream of attacks.

"It worked... I'm gonna keep pushing...!"

"Awooooh!"

Loading a darkness stone into my gun, I activated my support. If electrical attacks worked, then the black lightning the darkness bullets unleashed should hurt, too.

"Eat this!"

> Arihito activated Attack Support 2 → Support
  Type: Darkness Bullet
> Cion activated Bind Attack 1 → Hit ★Roving
  Tempest Demon Rabbit
★Roving Tempest Demon Rabbit was Bound and
  Electrocuted
> Melissa activated Helm Splitter → Destroyed
  section of ★Roving Tempest Demon Rabbit
Electrocuted status extended
> Elitia unleashed accumulated Scarlet Trails
Activated 29 stage attack

"SHAHGYAAA...!"

Cion and Melissa's successive attacks both found their marks. Elitia then sheathed her sword, and innumerable gashes instantly slashed at the Demon Rabbit, which reeled back.

That Helm Splitter—what did Melissa's huge kitchen knife destroy?

Whatever it was flew through the air, and Seraphina caught it.

"A sealing horn. With this removed, the monster has gained even more transformational capabilities."

The thing had fallen in my blind spot, so I couldn't make it out, but Ariadne explained it to me.

Transformation... Don't tell me...!

"Ari-poo, I'm gonna go nex— Huaah?!"

"Everyone, back away from that thing!"

I held Misaki back just as she went in for the attack. Now horn-less, the Demon Rabbit had enveloped itself in some sort of sphere that was crimson like blood. It then clawed through the bloody bubble as if being reborn—and emerged as a four-limbed humanoid creature.

◆Current Status◆
> ★Roving Tempest Demon Rabbit lost its Memory Sealing Horn
> ★Roving Tempest Demon Rabbit transformed into ★Stray Strada

As if we didn't have enough on our hands with a powerful Named Monster, it had now transformed—into a humanoid.

Should we try to get to it while it's still stirring, or retreat with all we've got?

"......!!"

That's when I heard her breathing directly in my head: Theresia, invisible thanks to her Active Stealth skill.

◆Current Status◆
> Theresia activated Sneak Attack ⟶ Damage to ★Stray Strada doubled
> Theresia activated Butterfly Frolic ⟶ Increased number of attacks
> Theresia activated Sneak Attack

A pale blue light enveloped Theresia's Razor Sword for the attack. Clearly, she had decided we needed to stop the monster in its tracks now.

"?!"

◆Current Status◆
> ★Stray Strada activated Coward's Hearing ⟶
  Detected Theresia's Active Stealth
> ★Stray Strada activated Naked Sword Snatch ⟶
  Nullified Active Stealth

The Demon Rabbit's new form—the Strada—sensed Theresia approach. And yet it didn't even look back at her, instead catching her drawn sword between two fingers and rendering her Butterfly Frolic moot.

Misaki looked at me. Without a word, I knew what she was thinking. She had a skill up her sleeve that could protect Theresia before the Strada delivered its own strike. However...

"Haaaaah!!"

◆Current Status◆
> Seraphina activated Surging Wave Advance and
  Shield Slam
> ★Stray Strada activated Shock Absorber ⟶
  Nullified knockback from Shield Slam

"Kh...!"

Seraphina rammed her body into the Strada to no avail: It didn't so much as twitch, much less present an opportunity for attack. Now both Seraphina and Theresia rushed to put some distance between themselves and the enemy, but it wasn't going to be easy to get out of its range.

"...※α≠Ω"

The Strada said something—something that definitely sounded like words. But it meant nothing to me.

"Atobe, if you please…!"

◆Current Status◆
> ★Stray Strada activated Moon Drill
> Kyouka activated Mirage Step ⟶ Evaded attack

Igarashi hadn't leaped to attack, but to evade the Strada's strike. In that split second, there was no time to think.

"Elitia—it's time!"

Our swordswoman had already gotten a running start, aiming for the instant after the Strada's attack to bust out her next big move—the one she'd decided the moment called for.

It's now sink or swim… Just get us out of this pinch…!

"≠Ω…!"

◆Current Status◆
> Arihito activated Attack Support 2 ⟶ Support
  Type: Force Shot: Dolls
> Elitia activated Star Parade and Luminous Flow
> ★Stray Strada activated Machine Gun Block

"Haaaaah!"

A shower of blows and blocks ensued at terrifying speeds, the ground shaking violently with every crash of sword and fist. Attack Support wouldn't work while the monster had its Machine

Gun Block activated. But Elitia knew well enough not to try the same thing twice.

"Unleash your powers, Antares!"

```
◆Current Status◆
> ELITIA activated LIBERATION ⟶ Unlocked
  ANTARES's capability: SCARLET SHADOW BLADE
> LUMINOUS FLOW partially penetrated MACHINE GUN
  BLOCK
> 27 stages of LUMINOUS FLOW hit ★STRAY STRADA
Added 27 SCARLET TRAILS
> ELITIA activated additional attacks
18 stages hit
Added 18 SCARLET TRAILS
```

Elitia's slashes overcame the Machine Gun Block, leaving pink gashes in their wake as they overtook and pierced the Strada's defenses.

"—?!"

The Strada silently cried out. The fact that Elitia's sword had found its mark meant my support would also work. In a matter of seconds, my manipulation stone, which shone most when used with a plethora of attacks, accumulated incredible power.

```
◆Current Status◆
> ATTACK SUPPORT 2 activated 45 times ⟶
  Accumulated ★STRAY STRADA manipulation
  points
> ELITIA unleashed accumulated SCARLET TRAILS
```

```
Activated 45 stage attack
Accumulated ★STRAY STRADA manipulation points
Negotiation now possible
> MANIPULATION STONE was destroyed
```

"Arihito, the enemy's acting differently…!" Suzuna cried.

This is nothing like all the times the stone's worked so far… It must be because the enemy's at such a high level…!

If we continued this combat, we'd risk injuring one or more of our party members before our battle with the Simian Lord. But if we had a chance to end the fighting now, I had to seize it.

"Leave us, Strada!"

```
◆Current Status◆
> ARIHITO requested ★STRAY STRADA to abandon
  battle ⟶ ★STRAY STRADA complied
```

"…Wh-what? That, uh…person? just froze like an ice pop…," said Misaki.

"You're successfully negotiating…with such a formidable monster…," Seraphina murmured after checking her license to get a handle on the situation.

The Strada looked down at Theresia, who still had her sword and shield at the ready. Then it spoke once more.

"……"

Did Theresia understand what it said? I couldn't be sure, but it did look as if the monster had communicated something. Theresia walked over to us, pointed at the Strada, then turned to Seraphina.

"That monster... Did the Strada say something?" I asked.

Theresia nodded. As soon as Seraphina held out the horn, we could tell the Strada fixed its gaze on it.

"Does it want the horn back...?"

"If we hand it over, won't it just go back into super-rage mode...? But I guess we can't exactly get it to run off home like this, huh?" Misaki wondered.

"Atobe, it looks like your powers are letting you talk to it. Maybe it could give us something in return if we give back the horn?"

"Mr. Atobe, have a look at your license," said Seraphina. "A new notification has appeared."

```
◆Current Status◆
>  ★STRAY STRADA has requested MEMORY SEALING HORN
   → Proposed conditions: Anything within
   ★STRAY STRADA's ability to offer
```

"Anything...? Then can we ask it to, like, join our side, too?"

The Strada must've heard Misaki's question, because it shook its head. I took that to mean the manipulation stone had gained some traction, but not enough for us to use it for that. Looking at the monster now, I could see that though it was covered in fur reminiscent of the Demon Rabbit, it now very closely resembled a human woman. A small wound remained where it had just lost its horn, but even that was already beginning to close.

"I'd like you to tell us where we can find Holy Stones, if you know... We came to this labyrinth to look for them."

I figured our best bet was to ask residents of the labyrinth where to go, though I could only test that theory now that we'd opened a means of communication.

The Strada turned its back to us without an answer. It walked over to the path skirting the ridge, then suddenly slid down the slope.

◆Current Status◆
> ★Stray Strada activated Rabbit Tornado ⟶
  Destroyed the terrain

An explosive blast powerful enough to shake the hills next assaulted our ears and took us off guard. Soon after, the Strada leaped back up to the top of the cliff and looked at us.

"Well...no wonder Vanessa and her party couldn't find anything after looking here," Elitia said, sighing.

When Lynée said we might find what we sought on the first floor, she'd only meant the possibility existed. But clearly, that didn't mean we'd find it easily.

A cave had opened up halfway down the steep slope the Strada had slid down. Was it trying to show us where to find Holy Stones, or... It didn't look like a trap, at least. Seraphina tried to return the Strada's horn, but the monster shook its head. Apparently, it wouldn't accept the horn until we found our Holy Stones.

"They say, 'Nothing ventured, nothing gained,' but...are we sure we're not venturing into a trap?"

Igarashi had a point, but we didn't have time to be indecisive.

We headed down the unmarked path that the Strada pointed out for us and into the cave partway down the cliff face.

Part III: Big Lotto

The Strada's skill had left the ground loose, so we took extra care as we descended the steep slope. We clung tight to the cliff surface as we moved down to the cave entrance.

"Yeesh, just looking down makes me go all numb... You doing okay, Kyouka?" Misaki asked.

"I-I'm fine. As long as we're careful, we'll manage..."

"Everybody, watch your step!" I called.

◆Current Status◆
> ARIHITO activated MORALE SUPPORT 1 ⟶ Party members' morale increased by 13

"Thank you, Arihito," said Suzuna. "A boost in morale means even high places aren't so scary anymore, it seems."

Suzuna and Misaki had gone bouldering back in Japan, and it showed. They proceeded across the cliff face relatively quickly. It was Igarashi I had to worry about—and sure enough...

"Eeek...!"

...!!

"Yikes… Are you okay, Igarashi?"

"Y-yeah…thanks… Sorry. I should've been more careful."

"Don't worry about it. Trust me—I'm not so good with heights, either."

As soon as I saw her lose her balance, I'd caught hold of her firmly. Then I'd used Yoshitsune's Leap to jump through the air and drop her off safely at the mouth of the cave.

"Ngh…!"

Next, it was Seraphina's turn to tumble—she'd lost her balance under the weight of her equipment. I didn't have time to think through how to save her; I teleported behind her and used Yoshitsune's Leap once again.

"Mr. Atobe, forgive my carelessness…"

"N-not at all. We should've distributed all that heavy gear more evenly."

"My training included climbing under a heavy loadout. I was so sure I could manage, but I was too confident and got careless."

I felt pretty exhausted all of a sudden—perhaps because I'd spent so much magic power in so little time. Right then, Theresia fished a potion out of her bag and handed it to me.

"……"

"Thanks, Theresia."

"We should rest here for a while before heading into the cave. It's bigger than I thought."

"Woof!"

Melissa and Cion came up behind me, looking concerned, but I'd drunk Theresia's potion and was already feeling less worn out by the minute.

The Strada looked toward us from a short distance away. I assumed it was keeping watch until we found the Holy Stones we sought.

At first, I thought about calling on the Harpies to help carry us, but they were afraid of the Strada, so I quickly canceled their summoning. Their fear seemed more visceral than ours.

"These are the Tremulous Foothills... I'm starting to think it's the Strada's ground-alteringly powerful attacks that make them so tremulous."

"It's certainly possible. Though I thought it might hint at the cave underground."

"It appears a lot more expansive than we imagined... Oh, what's that? Is it what they call lightmoss?"

"It's pretty dark in the cave, but it looks like we can at least enter safely. I hope I can at least find a way to make myself useful in here, since I couldn't manage anything before..."

"No need to get flustered. Let's start off by finding some light in this darkness!"

```
◆Current Status◆
> Raiding previously unexplored territory
```

```
> Chance of monster sighting: Unknown
> Presence of area effects: No skills to
  assess
> Caution: Sandy soil present
```

The cave mouth itself wasn't that spacious, but as soon as we stepped inside, we found the floor slanted downward toward a remarkably wide area.

I was a little concerned that the cave air might be filled with moss spores or something else that might inflict status ailments— but thankfully, it wasn't an issue at all. Far from it, in fact; for some reason, the air was refreshingly chill and pleasant.

"Ahhh, that's nice, isn't it? ...Wait a second. All those rocks over there look just like the ones here, but...is it just me, or are they all glowing?"

"Surely that's just lightmoss blooming... They can't all be Holy Stones, can they?"

"Misaki, why don't you give Big Lotto a try?"

"Should I? 'Kay! I'll try headin' over by that rock."

"I'm going with you. The rest of you, please stay here until we're sure that it's safe," said Seraphina. "Mr. Atobe, the mattock, if you will."

I handed her the Dwarf's Mattock. As soon as I had, Cion came over and circled around Misaki.

"Woof!"

"Huh? You're gonna give me a ride? For real? Your back's all super-fluffy and stuff..."

Cion let Misaki climb up onto her back, and they headed off toward a group of rocks that all had similar shapes.

I don't get the feeling there are any enemies nearby. Still, we don't know what the monster appearance rate here is. It wouldn't be unusual for something to pop up at any moment.

I prepared my slingshot and got ready to act the moment anything went wrong. Misaki looked back in my direction to make sure everything was in order, then set about activating her skill before Seraphina started in on the rocks with the mattock.

"Here goes! *Big Lotto!*"

```
◆Current Status◆
> MISAKI activated BIG LOTTO ⟶ Chance of
  finding rare items increased
```

With Misaki's Big Lotto skill in effect, Seraphina picked one rock out of many and swung the Dwarf's Mattock at it.

"...!"

```
◆Current Status◆
> SERAPHINA utilized DWARF'S MATTOCK ⟶ Destroyed
  LARGE ROCK LUMP G
```

The mattock, being magical, immediately cracked the lump of stone with the first piercing blow. The rock came apart to reveal several metallic masses inside.

```
◆Newest Acquisitions◆
> Heaven steel ore x3
> Crystium fragment x2
> Sterling Silver Sand x1
> Lightmoss x10
```

"If we just do this, it'll be a cinch to figure out which rocks to hit!" said Misaki.

"Mr. Atobe, there don't appear to be any Holy Stones among the materials we found."

"Gotcha. How is your magic power holding out, Misaki?"

"Just fine! Matter of fact, I'm gonna try using Big Lotto one more time! Here goes… *Big—*"

At that instant, I saw something strange.

The glow from the lightmoss grew faint, and the inside of the vast cave went dim. There were many mossy boulders in the cave, and all of them looked more or less the same, except…

Wait a second… Did that rock just…?

```
◆Current Status◆
> ARIHITO activated HAWK EYES ⟶ Detected ?ROCK
  LUMP's hidden ability
```

"Seraphina! Misaki! Get away from that rock—now!"

"Huh? Whaaaaaat?!"

```
◆Current Status◆
> ?ROCK LUMP's camouflage was lifted ⟶ ?ROCK
  LUMP was revealed to be DEEP EATER
```

> Deep Eater activated Gluttonous Gape → Target:
Misaki, Cion

The great, mossy boulder split open to form a mouth, gaping
before Misaki's eyes.

*An enemy that camouflages its true form... We should've seen
that coming!*

"GAAAAAAH!!"

"Eeeeeek...!"

"Misaki, take cover!" shouted Seraphina.

I've gotta slow it down, even if just for a moment!

◆Current Status◆
> Arihito activated Attack Support 2 → Support
  Type: Force Shot: Stun
> Deep Eater activated Super-Reaction → Action
  was canceled
> Seraphina activated Shield Slam → Target: Deep
  Eater
> Deep Eater activated Stone Stiffness → Parried
  Shield Slam
Nullified Stun
> Seraphina unequipped her shield

"Nngh...!"

Seraphina, with her shield firmly in place, had attempted to
charge the Deep Eater. However, it parried the blow with its stony
body. The Deep Eater wasn't even stunned. Seraphina's Mirrored

Shell Pavis went sailing through the air; until that moment, I couldn't even have imagined her losing hold of her shield.

Elitia broke into a sprint. Igarashi began casting a spell. Suzuna had an arrow nocked on her bow.

"Seraphina...!"

◆Current Status◆
> Deep Eater activated Armor Break ⟶ Damaged
  Seraphina's Guardian's Mail +4

"...!!"

It's no use... It's too tough!

"Haaaaaaugh!!"

Elitia chose her fastest skill and set about attacking the Deep Eater. However, as far as I could tell from its characteristics, attempting even one melee attack on it was a very risky proposition.

Would freezing even work on a monster made of stone? I had no clue. But I knew that I had to put a stop to its movement for at least a second.

Please, please work!

◆Current Status◆
> Arihito activated Attack Support 2 ⟶ Support
  Type: Vine Shot
> Elitia activated Comet Raid ⟶ Added Sword
  Barrier
> Elitia activated Slash Ripper

```
> Deep Eater activated Stone Stiffness ⟶ Parried
  Slash Ripper
```

Our attacks were completely negated—even Elitia's Antares couldn't land a successful hit. However, if she'd chosen Liberation, which would have taken more time to activate than Slash Ripper, the Deep Eater would have focused its attacks on Seraphina or Misaki instead.

Just as the name suggests, the Deep Eater had a mouth big enough to terrify even other monsters—a mouth that it stretched wide open. Its arms, with large claws on the ends, were now in motion; it had four unusually powerful limbs that served to support its massive body. It stepped forward on its two forelimbs...or at least attempted to.

```
◆Current Status◆
> Deep Eater was Bound by Vines
Action canceled
```

"Now! Break away from it!"

"Woof!"

```
◆Current Status◆
> Arihito activated Outside Assist
> Cion activated Hit and Run and Heat Claw ⟶
  Hit Deep Eater
> Deep Eater continued to be Bound by Vines
```

"GUGAHHH!!"

Cion rained Heat Claw strikes down on the Deep Eater. Even if her claws themselves couldn't scratch its rocky surface, the attack's fire attribute got through.

"Forgive me…!" said Seraphina.

"Don't worry! Now's our chance to regroup. That thing holds up too well against melee attacks… We'll give long-range attacks a shot!"

The Deep Eater's Super-Reaction skill posed a serious threat to our frontline combatants. We couldn't risk having any more of their equipment destroyed. The question was, how effective would long-range attacks be? We couldn't rule out the possibility that the Deep Eater had counterattacks for distance attacks, too. In that case…

We had to act before it could react. That meant we'd have to borrow some firepower from a certain monster who'd put us through a hard battle before.

Part IV: Rumbling Meteors and Azure Flame

The Deep Eater sort of resembled a turtle with an abnormally developed head and hind legs. It looked like it broke the laws of nature just to maintain balance, especially with its mouth, which was large enough to swallow an adult human whole.

What did it need a mouth that big for anyway? The cavern

appeared to be a closed space, but assuming the Deep Eater hunted somewhere, it was entirely possible that the subterranean space had another exit that led somewhere else.

"Here it comes, Arihito!" Elitia called.

"GAAAAAAH!!"

◆Current Status◆
> Deep Eater broke free of Vines
> Deep Eater activated Howling Quake → Area effect increased by 1 stage

"…What's going on?!"

"The whole cave is shaking… At this rate, it might collapse!"

The Deep Eater's roar rumbled throughout the cave. Maybe we'd discovered another reason they were called the Tremulous Foothills. It was amazing to think that a normal, non-Named Monster could use a skill strong enough to affect the very terrain.

"Atobe, behind you!"

Is it trying to block our only way out…?

The path that we'd taken down into the cave was already unstable, thanks to the Strada's skills. On top of that, the Deep Eater's Howling Quake had caused the walls to collapse, leaving only a small hole in an otherwise blocked-off pathway.

"Mr. Atobe, I must buy you some time…"

"No, Seraphina—fall back. It's too dangerous without your armor!"

"But—!"

"I've got another way to stop it... Come out, now!"

◆Current Status◆
> Arihito summoned Slow Salamander A and Slow Salamander B
> Arihito summoned Mage

"?!"

Using my Summoning Pendant, I called forth two Slow Salamanders and the Arachnomage. The Slow Salamanders essentially looked like even more giant versions of the Japanese giant salamander from back home; the Arachnomage was a monster that looked like a human woman from the waist up and a spider from the waist down.

"I see... So that's Arihito's plan!"

"Mr. Atobe, the Deep Eater...!"

The Deep Eater noticed I'd summoned monster backup; that same instant, its eyes—tiny, relative to its huge head—went red, as if they were bursting into flame.

"GUGAAAOOOOOOH!!"

◆Current Status◆
> Deep Eater activated Predatory Drive ⟶ Deep Eater transformed
> Deep Eater activated Surface Swimmer ⟶ Deep Eater's speed increased
Can now pass through terrain features

> SLOW SALAMANDER A and SLOW SALAMANDER B were
  frightened

The Deep Eater's arms transformed into finlike shapes. What followed was a nightmarish sight; it dove into the accumulated sand on the cave floor and started swimming through the ground as if it were water.

"KWOH..."

"Arihito, the salamanders are terrified...," said Suzuna.

The Deep Eater is a predator... No wonder the Slow Salamanders are so scared. It's their natural instincts kicking in!

"Ngh... Hit your target!" I cried.

◆Current Status◆
> ARIHITO activated ATTACK SUPPORT 2 ⟶ Support
  Type: VINE SHOT
> SUZUNA activated AUTO-HIT ⟶ Next two shots
  will automatically hit
> SUZUNA activated FORBIDDEN ARROW
> DEEP EATER activated SUPER-REACTION and
  BULLETPROOF 2 ⟶ Reduced damage from FORBIDDEN
  ARROW
Nullified Vines

It didn't connect. None of our attacks did. The Deep Eater kept plowing forward, as if mocking me for thinking that just because melee attacks were ineffective, ranged attacks would have to work.

"*I shall stop the monster. You need only speak my name, Master...*"

Under the circumstances, I couldn't call for Alphecca, but Murakumo could give me a hand. I grabbed the hilt of the sword on my back, knowing Murakumo would teach me a skill that might be able to stop the Deep Eater.

Elitia and Melissa were on the move. Cion was trying to help the Slow Salamanders, which were still frozen in fear, out of their jam.

Then, from somewhere beside me, a white hand reached out. It was Mage's hand—she wasn't trying to flee; rather, she was attempting to use a skill.

"*I will stop it... Now I know I can!*"

"Help me out here, Murakumo! Mage, I'll support you!"

◆Current Status◆
> ᴀʀɪʜɪᴛᴏ activated ᴀᴛᴛᴀᴄᴋ Sᴜᴘᴘᴏʀᴛ 2 ⟶ Support
   Type: Cʟᴏᴜᴅ Sᴛᴀɴᴄᴇ

The skill that Murakumo instructed me to use wasn't an attack—it was a stance, purely focused on defense.

"*As a sword,*" she said, "*the only role I can play is to cut foes down...or so I thought. In your hands, Master, I've learned that a sword can also defend!*"

"GAAAOOOOOOH!!"

◆Current Status◆
> Mᴀɢᴇ activated Wᴇʙ Sᴘɪɴɴᴇʀ

> Deep Eater activated Gluttonous Gape
> Deep Eater's speed decreased due to effects
  of Attack Support 2

"…!!"

Threads shot out of not only the Arachnomage's mouth, but her hands as well. She used Web Spinner to weave a spiderweb that, thanks to the defensive support effects of Cloud Stance, stopped the attack from the Deep Eater's gaping maw and caused it to gently decelerate.

"We're here, guys! Put your game faces on!"

Igarashi had taken that exact opportunity to come back—all the way back to where the Slow Salamanders were cowering motionlessly.

◆Current Status◆
> Kyouka activated Mist of Bravery ⟶ Fear
  status of Slow Salamander A and Slow Salamander B
  was removed

The Slow Salamanders, whose feelers had been sagging, were reinvigorated.

The Deep Eater was already slowed down; now, with the Salamanders' help, maybe the tide would turn…

Salamanders aren't strictly a prey species… They've got the strength to fight back, too!

"KWAAA…AHHH!"

"Misaki! Draw us a Joker!"

"O-okay! C'mon, cards, do me a solid!"

"My skill is derived from Cloud Stance... Master, please grant me permission to use it!"

"Take this!"

```
◆Current Status◆
> Arihito activated Attack Support 2 ⟶ Support
  Type: Drifting Cloud Meteor Thrust
> Arihito activated Cooperation Support 1
> Slow Salamander A activated Breath of Stagnant
  Water ⟶ Target: Midrange
Combined attack stage 1
> Slow Salamander B activated Breath of Stagnant
  Water ⟶ Target: Midrange
Combined attack stage 2
> Misaki activated Flame Joker ⟶ Inflicted
  Anger status on Deep Eater
Converted Deep Eater's weakness to flame
  attribute
Combined attack stage 3
> Combined attack Stagnant Resonance Wildcard ⟶
  Deep Eater's speed decreased three stages
Deep Eater was Concussed
```

"GAAAAAAHAAAHHH!!"

At the same instant that Misaki's card scored a direct hit on the Deep Eater, I hit it square in the jaw from a distance.

"Now's our chance!" said Elitia. "Arihito, the usual, please!"

"Right... I've got your backs, everyone!"
"Yes!"

◆Current Status◆
> Arihito activated Attack Support 1 and Cooperation
  Support 1
> Elitia activated Ultimatum → Attack power
  and speed increased
Added Scarlet Trails
> Elitia activated Luminous Flow → 63 stages
  hit Deep Eater
Added 63 Scarlet Trails
Combined attack stage 1
> Elitia activated additional attacks
42 stages hit
Added 42 Scarlet Trails
> Melissa activated Helm Splitter → Destroyed
  section of Deep Eater
Combined attack stage 2
> Kyouka activated Lightning Rage → Hit Deep Eater
Electrocution nullified
Combined attack stage 3
> Lightning Rage activated additional attacks
  → 3 stages hit Deep Eater
> Suzuna activated Forbidden Arrow → Hit Deep Eater
Combined attack stage 4
> Combined attack Luminous Lightning Rage Forbidden
  Split → 1,143 support damage
52 additional cooperation damage
> Deep Eater was Electrocuted

Since our enemy was slowed down, our multistage physical onslaught landed more direct hits than it would have otherwise. Every time Elitia's sword hit the Deep Eater's rocky hide, countless invisible blades shaved away at its strength.

That still wasn't enough to take it down...but one more push should do the trick!

"Everyone, please fall back!"

Seraphina's voice echoed through the cave. In an instant, a network of red-hot lines appeared all over the stony armor that encased the Deep Eater's entire body.

◆Current Status◆
> Deep Eater is about to use Shard Blast

Slowed down and backed into a corner, the Deep Eater had made its final choice: self-destruction. Even if we managed to avoid the blast itself, there was a good chance the shock wave would cause a total cave-in.

"Emergency escape measures may cause the loss of equipment. But the lives of my contract holders take precedence...," said Ariadne.

What she meant was that if the Deep Eater was about to self-destruct, as I imagined, she would teleport us to safety.

Assuming there were Holy Stones in this cave, it would be far more difficult to find them if it collapsed. Furthermore, if Ariadne were to teleport us out, we would likely lose our equipment... which was important.

Theresia... That's right. She's...

I hadn't felt Theresia's presence since the fight began. Of course, her usual modus operandi was to get herself into a key position and strike from the monster's blind spot.

But this time, it was different. Previously, I'd always at least gotten the feeling that she was there with us. Now I didn't feel her at all. Still, I knew she was there—she had to be.

"‼"

◆Current Status◆
> Theresia unleashed Mode Shift: Sand Clad
> Arihito activated Rear Stance ⟶ Target: Theresia

Theresia had been on the floor of the cave—burrowed into the sand, waiting for her chance to attack.

The Deep Eater's hindquarters were armored like the rest of it, but its protective layer wasn't as thick there as it was in the front. The effects of Misaki's Wildcard were another piece of the puzzle of our survival.

"Hold iiiiiit!"

"……‼"

"The twilight-piercing meteor blazes in twinkling flame."

◆Current Status◆
> Arihito activated Attack Support 2 ⟶ Support Type: Dazzling Flame Meteor Thrust
> Theresia activated Sneak Attack ⟶ Damage to Deep Eater doubled

```
> THERESIA activated BUTTERFLY FROLIC ⟶ Increased
  number of attacks
> THERESIA activated AZURE SLASH ⟶ Hit DEEP EATER
  6 times
Weak spot attack
Critical hit
> ATTACK SUPPORT 2 activated 6 times
> Defeated 1 DEEP EATER
```

With Butterfly Frolic active, Theresia dug into the slowed Deep Eater with dazzlingly rapid slash attacks. The Deep Eater's armor—which had seemed impervious to physical attacks up until that point—cracked before our eyes. And then...

The red-hot lines all over the Deep Eater's body cooled to black. The rumbling that shook the cave floor continued for a while, but soon it stopped, as did the cave-in.

"Haaah... Haaah... Did we finish it off in time?"

"We did...thanks to your hard work, Mr. Atobe."

Seraphina was walking straight toward me. As she spoke, my field of vision shook; before I knew it, I had collapsed.

"...Mr. Atobe, you've overexerted yourself, staying on your feet and using skills this whole time..."

"No," I said, "I'm not the only one who pitched in here. All of you did a great job."

Everyone was still wary of the Deep Eater, even though it now lay motionless. Sprawled out like this, it was massive; still, if we sent it to the Repository, we could probably get some useful materials out of it.

"Atobe, I think these little guys want to go somewhere..."

"...KWAH."

"Somewhere? Like, somewhere in this cave?"

When I looked around the cave, there didn't seem to be anything there except for the lumps of ore-filled rock. But Igarashi was right; the Slow Salamanders did indeed appear to be trying to head off in a particular direction.

"Woof!"

"Will you give them a ride, Cion?" asked Igarashi. "They may be a little slimy, but still..."

Relying on Cion's kind nature, we loaded the Slow Salamanders up onto her back. When the second one climbed up, it deftly positioned itself right on top of the first one. I guess that was natural salamander behavior.

That done, we proceeded as the Slow Salamanders led us. Soon we came to a crevice in the rock wall of the cave, though it was blocked off with moss and we couldn't see far through it.

"It looks like we can head through here... We should try to gather some Holy Stones first, though."

"Right," said Elitia. "We'd better look through what that monster dropped, too."

Now that the rumbling had stopped, it was time to prioritize our hunt for Holy Stones.

"None of these other rocks are gonna turn out to be monsters, are they...?"

"If a fight that frenzied didn't shake any of them into action, I think it's safe to assume they're just rocks."

It would have been nice to have a skill that could detect mimic monsters, but then, my Hawk Eyes and Theresia's Lookout 1 had missed the Deep Eater's camouflage. It was possible that its concealing effect had just been too strong.

In the end, though, none of the rocks we broke with the Dwarf's Mattock turned out to be hiding any monsters. All we had to do was sift through the scattered ore for Holy Stones.

Part V: Unexplored Territory

"Awright, here we go again! *Big Lot—*"

"Hang on."

"Fwuh? What's the big idea, Melissa?"

Since Seraphina's gear was broken, the task of mining had fallen to Melissa. She reached out to pass me the mattock as she spoke.

"This Dwarf's Mattock is only good for two more uses. If we use it any more, we'll have to charge it."

"There are limits to how much Seekers can mine without the help of specialists," said Seraphina. "Right now, we can't bring back any component clumps of rock as is."

She had a point. If any of the materials were main components of the labyrinth, it would be too risky to bring them outside with us without good reason. You could say it's part of the same workings that cause stampedes; labyrinths themselves are, in a way, self-contained.

"That means we need to make two successful strikes, then...," I observed.

"That last fight built up lots of morale... 'Kay, I'm ready to give it a shot!"

◆Current Status◆
> MISAKI activated FORTUNE ROLL ⟶ Next action
  will succeed automatically
> MISAKI activated BIG LOTTO ⟶ Special
  success: Guaranteed to find rare items

"Wh-whoa, that's a way different response than before!"

"Which rock should we break?" Melissa asked.

"See that one over there in the back? Go hit it!"

Melissa took the Dwarf's Mattock and lightly tapped the rock Misaki pointed out. It split apart with ease, revealing a white gleam that we hadn't seen at first glance, when it was just a mass of stone.

◆Newest Acquisitions◆
> Heaven steel ore x2
> Glowing gold x2
> Crystium fragment x2
> Sterling Silver Sand x1
> ★Holy Stone x2

"Atobe, look…!"

Igarashi gathered the white, glowing stone from the rubble and brought it over to me. This was it—the material we needed for a Curse Eater weapon.

"Great… We found it! And not only one stone, but two, even…"

"Since we've got some heaven steel ore, too, we might be able to have another weapon made…though we probably don't have the time for that."

"Still, we've got plenty of materials, and that's what matters. We've got more Sterling Silver Sand for compounding our equipment, too… What do you think? Should we leave one more use in the mattock, just in case?"

Igarashi articulated what I was puzzling over: whether we should use up our last charge in the Dwarf's Mattock to check one more rock.

"If we run into Yuuho, we could probably ask her how to recharge it. Then again, she said this was her spare, so it might be a one-time-use sort of thing."

"All right. Should we use Big Lotto and see if it finds another winning rock? If it does, we can decide to use the mattock then."

"Yeah, that sounds good. Do you have enough magic left, Misaki?" I asked.

"Enough for this, at least! *Big Lotto!*"

Misaki used her skill again, though it didn't produce the same results as the previous time.

"…Huh? My legs are all wobbly…"

"Misaki...are you okay?" asked Igarashi.

"Ah-ha-ha, I guess Big Lotto uses up more magic than I thought."

"It does when you use it over and over again like that. Hold still for a second," I told Misaki.

"Nnh... Oh, this is the same feeling I get when my magic recharges... I could really get used to this..."

"Um, well... Arihito is just making sure your magic is replenished. That's all—"

"Everything okay, Elitia?"

Elitia had apparently overheard while in the middle of drinking a magic potion. She'd started saying something but cut herself off.

"...Can I ask you to do me, too? I also used a lot of major skills in succession, and I guess it left me a bit worn out..."

"Receiving some of Atobe's magic does make you blush a bit, doesn't it? Then again, now that I think of it, drinking a magic potion should do the job instead."

"Y-yes, it should, but...since we've got the chance, I think it'd be better to let Arihito use his skills to replenish us."

Repeatedly using skills gives you a little bit of experience. That must be what she was getting at. Elitia turned her back toward me and moved her pigtails out of the way so I'd have direct access to her back.

"Okay... Here goes. *Charge Assist!*"

"...Thank you. I was right—that relieves the fatigue far better than recovering naturally."

"Don't say that, or everyone's going to want him to do it," said

Igarashi. "I mean, we're not even *that* worn out. There's no need to keep Atobe constantly on edge."

"Ha-ha... Well, we're not quite done in this labyrinth just yet, so I think it's good to make sure everyone's recovered. We need to make it down to the third floor, after all."

"In that case, it'd be best if I just headed down there and back myself. I'm all recovered now," Elitia said, winding up her arm to stretch it out. She was petite and delicate-looking, but the gesture made her look extremely capable.

Reaching the third floor of two labyrinths in District Five and registering three thousand or more contribution points at least twice—that was what it would take for us to qualify to explore five-star labyrinths.

I wasn't sure whether we'd hit three thousand points on this particular outing yet or not. It all came down to how our fight—and subsequent conversation—with the Strada would be evaluated; we wouldn't be able to say for sure that we'd hit three thousand without a little more fighting.

"...KWAH."

"Oh...I guess we kept you waiting. Is there something over there?"

I went over to the moss-covered passageway that the Slow Salamanders led us to and cleared the way with a Force Shot. Then we ventured through.

We eventually came to a fork in the path. One branch slanted upward; the other stayed mostly level. I figured that we could take the upward path if we needed another way out of the labyrinth. The air was chilly and slightly damp. The farther we walked, the louder the sound of flowing water grew.

"It looks like we're about to get some more visibility... Watch your step, everyone."

A beam of bright light cut through the cave. Elitia shielded her eyes as she stepped out of the cave.

"What is this...?"

We followed her out onto a high ledge—high enough that it looked like falling would be fatal. But despite the danger, looking out at the new view, I started to understand why so many people like mountain climbing.

"There's a watering hole at the base of the cliff...and it's small, but there's a waterfall, too," Igarashi noted.

"Hey, look! Don't those look kinda like our salamanders? They're just a different color."

◆Current Status◆
> Raiding previously unexplored territory
> Chance of monster sighting: Normal
> Presence of area effects: No skills to
  assess

"Unexplored territory, huh? I wonder if those beasts down there are the same as our Slow Salamanders, or at least a similar species of monster," I said.

"Discovering unexplored territory is guaranteed to be worth a lot of contribution points," Seraphina told me. "Add that to the battles we fought on the way here, and I'm quite certain we've met our quota already."

```
◆Monsters Encountered◆
★SLUMBERING WOOD LAKE DRAKE
Level 13
Neutral
Resistance Unknown
Dropped Loot: ???
SILENTREPS A
Level 10
Neutral
Lightning Damage Doubled
Dropped Loot: ???
SILENTREPS B
Level 10
Neutral
Lightning Damage Doubled
Dropped Loot: ???
```

"All three monsters look mild mannered, but that big one's still a dragon. It could be real trouble in a fight..."

"I guess our Slow Salamanders wanted to meet up with their friends..."

""KWAH!""

The two Slow Salamanders both cried out at the same time.

That was all they did, though. They stayed stacked on Cion's back, staring out at the loafing monsters for a moment, then tried to turn tail and look the other way.

"...I see. I bet that Deep Eater must have preyed on those Silentreps."

"That explains why our Salamanders were so afraid of it..."

Even monsters in labyrinths are part of an ecosystem. The Deep Eater only did what was necessary to survive; it's impossible to judge that as simply good or evil.

But Seekers have goals of their own, and to fulfill those goals, they have to defeat monsters. I wondered how the Slow Salamanders saw our behavior—a look into their beady little eyes didn't offer any insight into what they were thinking.

"Atobe, I think Mage is trying to tell us something..."

"Hmm? What is it, Mage?"

"..........."

Mage didn't say a word; she just pointed downward, toward the Slumbering Wood Lake Drake by the water. That's when I saw something that hadn't been there before. Something I had to use Hawk Eyes to make out.

◆Current Status◆
> ★Slumbering Wood Lake Drake dropped a ?Mask
Right of acquisition: Arihito's party

A monster dropped an item all on its own?

"Maybe it dropped it because we're here with the Slow Salamanders?" said Igarashi. "Or maybe it's a thank-you present for killing the Deep Eater?"

"There's a chance...it might be both," I replied.

Mage started moving at last—and immediately fell down the cliff. Or at least that's what I thought for a moment before I realized she was clinging to its sheer surface.

"Are you going to go get it for us?"

"............"

I peeped over the ledge to ask Mage the question; she nodded, then rode her threads down the cliff face in a flash. She passed between the monsters at the watering hole without incident and picked up the item the drake had dropped.

"I bet Mage has spent a lot of time thinking up stuff to do for Ari-poo..."

"Right... Some things get across even without words," Igarashi said, looking at Theresia as she spoke.

But Theresia didn't meet her gaze; she turned in another direction, as if to keep Igarashi's eyes off her.

"......"

"...Theresia?"

"I think she's probably just a little tired. How about calling it a day for now, Theresia...?"

We still had a few days ahead of us. It would be best for us to get out of the labyrinth for a bit. But before I could say any of that, Theresia grabbed hold of my sleeve and shook her head.

"...Gotcha."

Knowing that worrying too much about Theresia would just add to her burden, I couldn't think of any good words to say to follow up. But I knew that I couldn't overlook any small changes in Theresia's state. The hex was undoubtedly still eating away at her, and she had to bear that fear. I couldn't imagine what sort of pain she was going through.

"......"

Theresia let go of my sleeve and started stroking my arm as if to console me. Now I'd made Theresia worried about me... This wasn't the place to get into a slump.

Just then, Mage came back to give me the Lake Drake's present. It was a mask, shaped to cover one's face around the mouth, that appeared to be made of dragonscale.

"Looks like it provides plenty of defense," Misaki noted, "but it might be a biiit too flashy for practical use..."

"That's a risk I'm willing to take in order to maximize defensive power," said Seraphina.

"First things first, we should get it appraised. We could use a Return Scroll to leave, but I think we passed a route up and out of the labyrinth on the way here."

"That's right. That path looked pretty stable, too... But after all the changes in geography that happened earlier, we should investigate more closely."

"Woof!"

Since Mage and the Slow Salamanders had fulfilled their

duties, I released their summoning. Cion went ahead of us to lead the way as we walked back to the fork in the path and took the ascending branch this time.

"...We're back in the light again."

"I wonder where we'll step out this time," said Igarashi. "Come to think of it, do you think the Strada is still waiting for us outside the cave?"

That reminded me: We had to return the Memory Sealing Horn, or else. I wondered what the Strada had done after we'd been sealed inside the cave.

In the end, though, I'd worried over nothing. We left the cave to find the Strada leaning with its back against the wall by the entrance.

"We found the Holy Stones we were after. Here's the sealing horn back, as promised."

◆Current Status◆
> ARIHITO is recognized as the owner of the
  MEMORY SEALING HORN
> ★STRAY STRADA's status changed to friendly

"Huh... Uh, what just happened?"

I offered the horn, but the Strada refused to accept it. In fact, when I approached the Strada, it took my hand in its and started nuzzling it with its cheek.

"H-hey...," said Igarashi. "Don't tell me it's attached to you now..."

"Well, that item was a Memory Sealing Horn," said Suzuna. "Maybe that means that it sealed their memories away while it was on their head... Could that have something to do with it?"

I'd assumed that the horn was a natural part of the Strada's body. But if Suzuna's conjecture was accurate, the horn might have been attached in order to block the Strada's memory.

"The labyrinths are home to the kin of Hidden Gods, but many phenomena therein are yet unknown... Still, I too sense that this monster harbors no animosity."

Murakumo also seemed perplexed by this turn of events, but I supposed anything was possible.

"In that case...will you come with me?"

"You're taking the Strada along, Elitia?" I asked.

"That's right. All of you, wait at the labyrinth entrance."

"With Ellie and the Strada together, no matter what kinda monster they run into, there's gonna be an all-out super-brawl to see who's the strongest in the labyrinth!"

"That seems a little far-fetched...," I ventured. "Still, it'd be nice to get the Strada's help. I bet it knows a lot about this labyrinth, too."

"...H-huh? Hey, that tickles..."

The Strada rubbed its rabbit ears against Elitia to show how friendly it had become. Then it clenched its fist in camaraderie.

"We'll get through this as quickly as we can. Can you show us the way to the next floor?"

The Strada gave its ears a twitch—which seemed to be its way of saying yes. Elitia nodded back, grinning.

The two of them activated speed-boosting skills and took off so quickly, it looked like they were flying. In the blink of an eye, they were out of sight. Reflexively, I looked at the faces of the remaining party members; every one of them looked half-flabbergasted and half-impressed.

"It would be really helpful if the Strada joined forces with us for good...but that might be too tall an order," said Igarashi.

"If I were at the level to tame her, she'd be a real ace in the hole, even among all the monsters we can summon," I replied. "But I'm not quite there yet."

"It's a shame that we must rely on Ms. Elitia alone, but in terms of speed, I doubt there's another Seeker in the entire district who can keep up with her."

I wanted to rack up some more combat experience if possible, but I'd realized something while fighting the Deep Eater: As we were, every fight we got into with a monster in District Five still forced us into a risky situation.

"What do we do about your armor, Seraphina?" I asked. "We managed to salvage the scraps, at least..."

"As broken as it is, it'll take a long time to fix. We'll make use of whatever we can get at shops in town. We simply have to hope they have the right size."

Would we be able to find any equipment that matched up to Guardian's Mail +4? A greatshield might stand up to enemy attacks, but obviously, it's still best to have the highest defense possible in your armor, too.

Armor with rune slots would be ideal, but how realistic is that? We've found a lot of metal, but who knows whether it's enough to make a new suit of armor? Not to mention how long it might take.

Ideally, we'd end up with a complete set of powerful armor. If that wasn't possible, then we'd have to make do with the best gear we could get off the rack.

Now that we had Holy Stones, we'd order a Curse Eater weapon, too. All these thoughts of what we'd have to do next filled my brain as we walked back toward the labyrinth entrance.

CHAPTER 3

Gathering Power as the Hour Approaches

Part I: The Hex Resurfaces

We hadn't been waiting for Elitia and the Strada very long before they returned.

Time passes more quickly in labyrinths. The sun was already going down, and night was approaching. I wondered how things were outside the labyrinth.

"Thanks for taking the trouble, Elitia."

"Not at all... Just as I thought, the flow of time isn't stable here. We'd better find out exactly how much time has passed, and soon."

As long as you fight monsters and make your way through a labyrinth, your level increases—however, you have a certain time limit.

"Thanks for showing me the way, Strada... Will we meet again?"

The Strada didn't answer Elitia, but once more, its ears twitched in what looked like an affirmation.

We watched as the Strada turned and left. I wondered what the meaning was behind the name *Stray* Strada, and what had happened to this creature before. There was a lot I didn't understand. We left the labyrinth, praying that we'd meet the Strada again someday.

It was total night outside. The only light in our surroundings came from lampposts scattered here and there.

"Aw, this late already...? I feel like a mini Rip van Winkle over here," said Misaki.

"Yeah," I agreed. "We'd better head back to the inn for now. Theresia?"

Theresia was going through a change that I should have already noticed. She stopped in her tracks. I moved to be by her side and had started to speak, when suddenly—

"......!"

I felt something like a wave of electricity running through my whole body, which made me bend backward.

As Theresia turned around to look at me, I saw a clear pang of agony cross the part of her mouth peeking from her mask.

◆Current Status◆
> THERESIA became hostile due to effects of
  EVIL DOMINATION

```
> THERESIA attacked ─→ Hit ARIHITO
> THERESIA's karma rose
```

"Kngh…!"

A spray of red escaped from a shallow tear in my suit.

"……"

Theresia didn't follow up with another attack.

```
◆Current Status◆
> THERESIA resisted EVIL DOMINATION ─→ Resistance
  unsuccessful
```

She was struggling to stop herself. She had the blade of her sword angled toward herself but couldn't keep it there; it slowly pointed back toward me.

More than the pain coursing through my chest—more than anything—what really hurt was the regret I felt. Regret that I hadn't checked on how the hex on Theresia had progressed before taking her back into a labyrinth.

"Theresia!"

"H-hey, what gives? C-cut it out! Stop…!"

"Misaki, get down!" I yelled.

```
◆Current Status◆
> THERESIA attacked ─→ MELISSA defended
```

"……!"

"Theresia… Settle down… Please, snap out of it…!"

How were we supposed to defend ourselves against one of our own? This wasn't a simple status ailment like Confusion or Charm. My license told me that Theresia was now verified hostile, showing just how unnatural—and critical—the situation was.

I'd always thought that, no matter what happened, we could overcome it, just as we always had. That naive assumption of mine had invited this disaster.

"Theresia!"

"……!!"

"T-Theresia, I'm so sorry!"

◆Current Status◆
> Kyouka attacked ⟶ Theresia activated Dodge
> Theresia activated Reverse End ⟶ Target:
  Kyouka

A memory of Theresia pointing at her license to acquire that skill arose from the deep recesses of my brain.

Igarashi lashed out with the tip of her spear, but not with intent to hurt; she was only trying to stop Theresia. Theresia dodged and instantly moved to counterattack. Theresia's attacks were much, much more powerful than Igarashi's—so powerful that if they connected, they would leave critical wounds. But Theresia moved too quickly for Igarashi to even activate Mirage Step.

Just then, I saw a bright, silver light pierce the deepest darkness of the night.

"Haaaaaah!"

◆Current Status◆
> Kozelka activated Garm's Advance, Wandering Target
  Flare, and Weapon Hunt
> Nullified Theresia's counterattack
Theresia lost her weapon

"......"

Kozelka parried Theresia's blow with her thin sword. Theresia's Razor Sword went sailing through the air until Khosrow knocked it to the ground with a gauntleted hand.

◆Current Status◆
> Kozelka used Binding Bangles ⟶ Theresia was
  restrained

Kozelka bound Theresia's hands with what looked like a pair of large rings. Keeping her sharp eyes on the immobilized Theresia, Kozelka spoke.

"Status ailment or none, no demi-human can attack their allies in the middle of town and expect to keep their freedom. We're taking Theresia to the Guild."

"Wait a second, please," I begged. "Theresia—she's…!"

◆Current Status◆
> Theresia resisted Evil Domination ⟶ Theresia is
  no longer hostile

Theresia was still fighting the Evil Domination. Even Kozelka and Khosrow could tell that it hadn't taken complete control of her yet. Still, they continued to stare harshly at her and showed no intention of undoing her restraints.

"Look, Atobe," said Khosrow. "She's already done enough for us to bring her in. If anything, you're lucky that we happened to be on the scene. If we hadn't been able to stop her little rampage, you'd be looking at a lot worse than a few injuries."

"But...but surely Theresia hasn't done anything worth imprisonment!"

"Yeah, yeah, I know. She didn't mean any harm by it, am I right?"

"Khosrow..."

Khosrow grabbed hold of my arm and held me in check as he spoke, but I still wouldn't back down. I couldn't let them take Theresia away. At that hour, there weren't many bystanders in the area to see it, but Theresia had indeed turned on us and attacked in plain sight.

"...We're taking her in. Send a party representative to Guild Saviors headquarters, and we'll fill you in on what comes next."

With that, Kozelka and Khosrow left with Theresia in tow. My party looked to me; I couldn't leave them lost in their uncertainty.

"I'm going to the Guild Saviors HQ. I'll be back with Theresia for sure."

"...Very well, Mr. Atobe. We'll be waiting at the inn."

"Please get Theresia back safe...please. I'm so sorry I couldn't do anything..."

"There's nothing to be sorry about, Igarashi. You did your best not to hurt her. That's why Kozelka was able to step in."

"But what about you, Arihito...?" Elitia asked.

"Don't worry about me. It wasn't that bad. Theresia wasn't aiming to kill."

But I knew that wasn't the truth. The Simian Lord's domination had made Theresia attack me. She hadn't been acting from her own free will at all—which meant she had no say in how severely she attacked, for better or for worse.

"...!!"

As I split from the party and walked on, I checked my license. What I saw made me so angry, I wanted to scream—but all I could do was glare up at the heavens.

◆Theresia's Status◆
▶ Evil Domination progression: 46
> Progression speed increased due to defeat of Deep Eater under Cursed status

Kozelka and Khosrow were waiting for me in the conference room at the Guild Saviors headquarters.

"...My apologies; our response was quite sudden," said Kozelka.

"We had been dispatched to patrol the district, but that isn't the only reason we were on the scene. The other reason, Mr. Atobe, was that we'd heard a report that you and your party were out seeking."

"So you're saying...you had us marked?"

"Word around here has it that you're gonna go toe-to-toe with the Simian Lord in the Blazing Red Mansion," Khosrow told me. "Thing is, we had no idea how much progress you've made, so we got the okay to investigate for ourselves... 'Course, if nothing had happened, we would've sat tight until the day actually came."

"Sorry for not keeping you guys in the loop. Today we went out to the Tremulous Foothills to gather some materials we needed. We'll put our plan in motion as soon as we're ready."

"To think you're gonna qualify to seek in level-five labyrinths four days after arriving in this district... I knew there was something about your party that went beyond your levels."

Kozelka's expression hadn't changed, but I could tell she was speaking from the heart. Khosrow stood silently at her side.

"Well, we do have a couple crucial high-level pillars in Elitia and Seraphina. But still, each battle we get into has me feeling like we're walking a tightrope."

"Most parties who take on the Blazing Red Mansion are made up of level-ten Seekers or higher—level nine at the least. But even in a labyrinth that tough, I'd expect your party has a fighting chance. It's not too reckless for you to take on District Five labyrinths… Third Class Dragon Major Dylan, Captain Nayuta, and others vouch for you."

"Thank you for saying so. But helping Theresia and rescuing the Seekers the Simian Lord has subjugated are all that matters to us. If we can't manage those, none of that praise means anything."

"…Theresia appears to be under the influence of Evil Domination. We are keeping her in a cell for now. We can't simply hand her over, not even to you, Mr. Atobe."

"She got hit with that hex when you and your crew ran into the Simian Lord in the Blazing Red Mansion last time, huh?"

Khosrow and Kozelka knew the details of the situation, but that didn't mean they'd release Theresia any sooner. If anything, Theresia being hexed in such a way was grounds for them to keep her under lock and key for even longer.

"We've left the Simian Lord alone because taking it down would mean injuring or killing the Seekers under its control. It's also not likely to cause a Stampede, which is another argument for letting it be," Kozelka explained.

"…However, in the Guild Saviors bylaws, there's a clause that classifies Seekers who are subordinates of a monster as monsters themselves. There's those who take advantage of that clause to rob those Seekers of their equipment. That's not a violation of any rule. Personally, though, I'd say a human's a human, even if a monster's controlling them—and that means there's probably some way to save them. But that might just be my ego talking."

"We'd prioritize incapacitating them without killing them. Or maybe we'd just focus on the boss," I said. "If we take down the Simian Lord, all the people under its control would be freed. At least I think that's a definite possibility."

"At present, no one else is making a concentrated effort to defeat the Simian Lord. Not even the White Night Brigade consider the Simian Lord a viable target for extermination, and they're a once-in-a-generation party that happens to be staying in District Five."

I wondered whether the White Night Brigade had already reached their goal in the Blazing Red Mansion when Rury got captured by the Simian Lord—or if they'd decided the risk was too great and given up on clearing the labyrinth then. I still didn't know.

"Keep that in mind. The monster you've decided to go up against is such bad news, even the White Night Brigade won't touch it," said Khosrow. "On top of that, you're planning on trying not to kill any of the Seekers under its control—its own private army. As if that weren't enough, judging by your party's overall MO, you're more than willing to get hurt yourselves."

"...I get that you think it's too much to manage. But still—"

"Listen, Mr. Atobe. I want you and your party to understand this. Let's say you end up having to kill the Seekers that the Simian Lord has doing its bidding. You should not let it weigh on your conscience... But if you insist on holding yourselves to that condition, even in the middle of battle, well... That's something worth respecting."

"Look, I don't feel like going up against a formidable opponent and getting totally wrecked, but here we are, so I gotta ask again. Even if it might get me fired from this job. How 'bout letting us get a taste of the action?"

"Khosrow..."

"I've got the authority to release Theresia. You'd regret leaving her in a cell while you went off into a labyrinth, wouldn't you, Mr. Atobe? If so, allow me to join your party for a while."

"...Huh?" I blurted out in confusion. I couldn't see how this connected to what we'd been talking about at all.

Khosrow was all smiles; when I looked over at Kozelka, she was covering her mouth with her hand.

"As a third-class dragon captain, I can assume managerial control over Seekers who're deemed to need observation. I can even allow certain troublemakers to accompany any party I'm a member of—with the rest of the party's approval, that is. Even if those troublemakers happen to be demi-humans."

I knew it was probably best for Theresia to stay where she'd be safe. But I also couldn't help wanting to get her out of that cell as quickly as possible. I wrestled with that contradiction.

"If you decide to leave Theresia here, there's a chance she'll be sent back to District Eight. From there, she'd be stripped of her seeking rights and sent off to a correctional facility... But as long as Kozelka is with Theresia, nobody can interfere with her. Your party will still bear the risk of having her around, though. That's just something you'll have to put up with."

"Khosrow, you— No, now is not the time. How does all of this sound to you, Mr. Atobe?"

I couldn't think of any reason why Kozelka and Khosrow would go through so much trouble for us—and yet they were. They spoke of it like it was the obvious choice. I felt something hot welling up inside me and put a hand to my chest. Kozelka's eyes subtly widened as she watched me.

"Are your injuries bothering you, Mr. Atobe?"

"No...it's nothing, really. I'm not the one who's suffering here."

"I think you undersell yourself too much, Atobe. But I also think that's how you end up with so many people in your corner. Look—you've even got me and Kozelka wrapped up in all this."

"I wouldn't say we're 'wrapped up.' We're cooperating because we want to."

"Thank you... Both of you. Truly..."

"Save the thanks for later. The real hard stuff's just getting started. But hey, when it's all over, we'll have plenty to talk about over drinks."

Khosrow extended his right hand. As I reached out to shake it, Kozelka stood up and walked toward us.

"We're heading into the Blazing Red Mansion tomorrow," I said.

"Right. So for today...please take Theresia home and get all the rest you need."

"We'll stay in the same inn as your party tonight," added Khosrow. "In two separate rooms, of course."

"I don't think that's really any concern of Mr. Atobe's... You must learn to tighten your lips, Khosrow, or I'll be leaving you behind."

"Whoops, sorry 'bout that, Third Class Dragon Captain, ma'am."

Kozelka stared daggers at Khosrow but spared him any further scolding as she left the room.

"All right, I'll show you to Theresia's cell. Follow me."

They were holding Theresia in the third basement of the Guild Saviors headquarters. Nothing that I'd feared had come to pass; Theresia sat calmly behind the iron bars of her cell, hands on her knees.

"Good to see you, Dragon Sergeant."

The male Guild Saviors on guard duty saluted Khosrow. The lower-ranking members bowed with a hand pressed to their chests, while the senior officers saluted by raising their right hands.

"This Seeker is coming with me. Third Class Dragon Captain Kozelka authorized her release."

"But, sir, after this demi-human's summary proceedings, she's to be sent back to the District Eight Mercenary Office, where she came from..."

"Plans have changed. I've got documentation from Captain Kozelka, if you need it."

"...R-roger, sir. I had no idea you had such an, er, interest, Dragon Sergeant..."

"An interest in what, exactly?"

"N-nothing, Dragon Sergeant... Never mind..."

Flustered by Khosrow's intimidation tactics, the guard opened Theresia's cell.

However, Theresia showed no signs of coming out. With Khosrow's permission, I entered the cell myself and extended a hand to her.

"Come on, Theresia. Let's go."

"......"

I was only there to pick Theresia up. I knew that she was no longer hostile. I wasn't afraid of her at all. Everything was exactly as it'd always been between us. I smiled at Theresia to prove it to her.

At last, Theresia reached up to me. With her hand in mine, she stood up.

Theresia's hand was shaking, and I understood why. Because she was the Theresia I knew.

On our way out of the cell and back up to the surface, Khosrow spoke so only I could hear him.

"Sorry, Atobe. Thing is, even among the Guild Saviors, some folks are biased against demi-humans. I wouldn't recommend leaving Theresia anywhere in their sights for long. I tell ya, even among those of us fighting for the good of the Labyrinth Country, there's still folks like that."

"So that's why you called for me so quickly, then? She didn't even end up staying here overnight."

"Demi-human or not, she's a young lady. She'd be awful sad and lonely, having to stay in a place like this... Heh. Sorry for laying on the straight-shooter act."

"Not at all... You're the one who told me to keep my cool. Ever since I first came to the Labyrinth Country, I've met a lot of reliable people. That's how I've managed to come as far as I have."

"And I'm one of those people, huh? I mean, maybe... Nah, you're just killin' me with kindness here."

Khosrow didn't say anything else as he escorted us to the exit on the ground floor of guild headquarters. Kozelka was waiting for us there.

And not only Kozelka. I caught sight of another familiar face beside her.

"Luca...!"

"You sure kept me waiting... Oh, I suppose this is hardly the place for putting on airs. How has life been without me, Arihito? Not too difficult, I hope."

It was Luca, all right—that same comic extravagance, short hair, and slender, androgynous frame. Every last detail was exactly the same as when I'd met him in District Seven.

"That's Atobe for you," said Khosrow. "Friends all over the place. Just overflowing with personal magnetism, eh?"

"Oh, I can see this Guild Savior here is no ordinary man—it's written all over him! Arihito, not to be a bother, but could you fill me in a bit on the way to the inn? I've asked Kozelka here, but she hasn't quite gotten me all the details."

"Of course. But first, Luca, what brings you to District Five?"

I didn't think I needed to finish the question, though; my eyes told me the whole story as they fell on the large suitcase at Luca's side.

"I couldn't fix the raiment that Madoka asked me about just yet, on account of I didn't have the right materials...but I did finish the suit. I was basically *obsessed* with getting it made, and I suppose I managed to finish in the nick of time. Looks like you could use a new suit right about now, hmmm?"

I'd ordered a brand-new suit from Luca—one made with materials from the Thunder Head and Darkness Blitz—and it was ready. That meant I'd get a defensive boost from my suit itself for the first time in a while.

"So you're a tailor, eh, Luca? Name's Josh Khosrow—just another Guild Savior nobody."

"Oh, I know that look! You've got 'I should order a suit of my own' written all over your face. It just so happens that Arihito's got me on retainer, so I'm sure I can squeeze you in next time my hands are free."

Luca had clearly wasted no time in asking Kozelka about me after arriving. I couldn't help but be impressed that she hadn't intimidated him.

"Looks like you've made all sorts of acquaintances."

"Y-yeah. I've worked with Luca since we met back in District Seven."

"He looks like he could help boost your fighting strength, too. Shall we ask him for assistance?"

It was true—Luca's true strength was plain to see at first glance. I wouldn't put him on the front lines of any battle, but he could likely hold his own in a fight in a support role. As Kozelka had implied, though, it would come down to Luca's own intentions.

Part II: Getting a Boost

We returned to the inn to find Igarashi and the rest gathered in the living room, having changed their clothes. It turned out that Ceres had called them together—and someone I hadn't expected to see was there with them.

"Hey, Arihito!"

"Lynée..."

Ceres pulled the brim of her conical hat down to cover her face. Steiner looked somewhat baffled in front of Schwarz, the scarecrow that Lynée had brought along.

"I figured I couldn't have you all drag yourselves out to my place again, so I came into town. I haven't been here in a while..."

"You say that like you stepped out on a whim, but you've kept yourself holed up out there for a while, haven't you?"

"Hmph. Maybe so, but I have my reasons... Now be honest, you're glad to see your old friend's face for the first time in ages, aren't you, Ceres?"

"*Old friend?* It's been so long, you're practically a stranger!"

When Ceres was with Steiner, she seemed mature beyond what her girlish looks would suggest. But with Lynée in tow, she was showing a side of herself I'd never seen before.

"I know Ceres is a jade... Are you from the same place as her, Lynée?"

"Yes, as it shakes out! I became a Seeker before Ceres did, and all those trials and tribulations led me to where I am today... Anyway, let's get started with those Holy Stones! Personally, I'd suggest you let Ceres handle them—she's better with them than I am."

"What are you talking about? ...Well, that's what I'd *like* to say. But Arihito here already knows that the two of us are about equally capable of the same things."

"Right... I'm sure you already know, Ceres, but to draw out the power of unique ores and add 'em to weapons, you need one of these—a transmitter pearl!"

"...So you got your hands on one, huh? It's been years since I last saw a transmitter pearl..."

"Found this one myself back in my seeking days. I figured I might never use it again, but, well, then I met Arihito here."

Lynée reached into the chest portion of her robe and pulled out a pendant—specifically a metal locket—containing a few gems. She removed one of the gems and passed it to Ceres. Seeing the two of them like that, I was struck by just how similar they looked. Both of them were jades, and thus they looked significantly younger than they actually were. Their hair was nearly the same flaxen shade. But the point of resemblance that made the strongest impression was their eyes, which were the exact same color.

"In order to keep your party's private information confidential, Mr. Atobe, we'll be leaving the room now."

"If anything happens, just call, and we'll be right back in a flash. If there's anything the Guild Saviors are good at, it's being on standby."

"Thank you! Really, you've got to let me thank you properly again—"

"Nonsense. In a way, you're just letting us do what we wanna do."

"The way Khosrow put that could use a little work...but we are hoping for you and your party's safety. That's all we ask—no thanks necessary."

"In that case, yours truly will be stepping out until you need me, too. I can't exactly smoke my you-know-whats indoors, can I?"

"Well, well, Luca! Looks like you brought the good stuff."

Luca and Khosrow had both pulled cigar cases out of their breast pockets. Kozelka drew a light but audible breath as she watched the two of them walk out of the room together.

"Um, if you don't mind, may I have a word?" Falma asked Kozelka.

"...Certainly. Lieutenant Seraphina, may I have some of your time later, then?"

"Y-yes, Third Class Dragon Captain. Roger."

Kozelka walked off with Falma. Soon we'd be heading off to Ceres's workshop; they would be waiting nearby, chatting until we returned. I knew that Kozelka and Khosrow hung back because of Theresia, but I imagined that there was little to worry about with the Binding Bangles on both of her wrists.

I wanted to get those off her—but I'd have to ask Kozelka to do that later. Of course, I would bear full responsibility for anything that happened afterward, but I wasn't sure whether saying so would be enough to get Kozelka to accept.

When we arrived at the workshop, Ceres set the transmitter pearl she'd received from Lynée down next to the Heaven's Stiletto.

"Hmm... This kind of sword, eh? No weapon for a soldier— only those with certain jobs can wield something like this. Are you sure this is the one?"

As a Rearguard, there wasn't any weapon or armor that I couldn't equip. But unless the weapon itself supported me as I wielded it, like Murakumo did, I couldn't hold a candle to any of the jobs that usually equipped it. Whenever possible, I wanted to make sure that weapons got into the hands of the party members who could use them best.

If none of our party members could equip the stiletto, we'd have had to search for a new Sorcery Tool to act as a base for a Curse Eater weapon. But with Madoka looking into it for us, we were able to determine the correct job for the gear.

"As a Rogue, Theresia can equip weapons like this one."

"In that case, we'll definitely need her with us to defeat the Simian Lord... Then again, participating in that battle—or getting close to the Simian Lord at all—might not be something Theresia can handle now..."

Elitia's misgivings made perfect sense. Theresia had attacked me before; the possibility remained that she might do it again if we fought the Simian Lord. The monster might well influence the corrosive progress of her hex. Given how far it had progressed already, there was a risk that she could instantaneously fall under the Simian Lord's control. With that in mind, it seemed clear that keeping Theresia in a safe location should be our top priority.

"With a Curse Eater weapon equipped, she's certain to land a hit. The question is, will Theresia be able stay on, you know, *the right side* long enough to do so?"

"......"

Theresia nodded at Ceres's question.

"As an outsider who hasn't known Theresia very long...I may have underestimated the strength of her feelings for you and your party, Arihito. But I can see clearly now. Those feelings will come in handy warding off the ill effects of the curse—at least at its worst."

"...Lynée, what exactly do you mean by *warding off*...?"

"I'm something of a hex worker myself, you know. I happen to know a few countermeasures for hexes. Consider my skills as a sort of insurance. I can't stop the hex from corroding her further, but I can make it inflict status ailments less frequently."

                    *   *   *

Lynée's voice dropped to a whisper, so faint it couldn't be heard. She mumbled something as she turned to Theresia with her palms outward.

◆Current Status◆
> LYNÉE activated BONDING INCANTATION ⟶ Success
THERESIA gained PSYCHE BARRIER 1

"...That should do it. It's rather rare for that skill to succeed, even in a party that's made it all the way up to District Five. And it's not something that can be used over and over again, mind you. At any rate, it needs you to be hexed to work at all!"

"Thank you very much, Lynée... For everything."

"Now, now. I can't let Lynée hog all the spotlight, can I?" Ceres said.

As Lynée watched on along with the rest of us, Ceres waved her hands over the Heaven's Stiletto and a Holy Stone.

"O sacred, shining stone! Let your power flow into this pearl, so that it may find harbor in a weapon true...!"

◆Current Status◆
> CERES activated EXTRACT ⟶ ★HOLY STONE's
  unique characteristics were extracted as a
  magic glyph
> CERES activated CONVERSION ⟶ Magic glyph was
  applied to HEAVEN'S STILETTO +4

The Holy Stone began to shine; its light was drawn into the transmitter pearl. The light in the pearl shone brighter and brighter until it finally took the form of a glowing glyph, which then drifted toward the Heaven's Stiletto and soaked into it.

```
◆★Gloria Stiletto +6◆
> Piercing attacks are more likely to
  inflict critical hits
> Attack power increased when a different
  weapon is equipped in each hand
> Attack speed increased
> Chance to avoid enemy attention increased
> Fitted with SILENT STONE
> Special Attack: Curse deals additional
  striking damage to a monster using hexes
Activates CURSE EATER when that monster is
  defeated
```

With the magic glyph engraved onto Heaven's Stiletto, it had a new name—likely because we'd used a starred material to upgrade it. I didn't think it had had the ability to decrease enemy attention before, either, so that must have been added as well.

"Phew... Good thing the upgrade was a success. If it'd been a failure, we would've lost the materials, too."

"*I guess Holy Stones are difficult for even you to work with, Master.*"

"At least we have a spare on hand in case of failure. Plus we could always ask Misaki to help out—she'd make success a sure thing."

"That'd be one way to do it... Honestly, Arihito, your party's just packed with interesting folks."

"Aw, that might be overselling me a bit..."

Misaki blushed. She couldn't use Fortune Roll in town, as a rule; Ceres would have to accompany us into a labyrinth for her to be able to do that. It seemed she might have to do exactly that eventually, just so we wouldn't lose any particularly precious materials.

"And with that, my debt to your party is paid, Arihito. Circumstances being what they are, I can't actually join you in combat, but someday I'd like to at least send Schwarz to help in my stead. So do please try to survive until then... I hope that's not too troublesome a request."

"Thank you, Lynée—and please, your well wishes are all we need. We definitely appreciate you teaching us how to remove the hex."

"...I do hope Theresia can be freed from it without succumbing to it. Now, Ceres, you take care, too... You and that armored apprentice of yours."

"May we accompany you as well, Mr. Atobe?"

"I'd like to ask you to secure our escape route, if you would. We'll handle fighting the monsters, but it'll be difficult for us to watch our own backs while we're storming the Simian Lord's stronghold."

"Certainly. We've fought along with you before, Arihito,

together with Luca. I can't say we've grown to the point since then where you could call on us anytime, but our levels have increased, at least."

Naturally, we couldn't let our supporters do anything too dangerous—but having allies behind us would make a big difference in our comfort levels when it came time to escape after defeating the Simian Lord.

"There. I've made a weapon that you'll need to free Theresia from her hex. I've also finished the Queen's Tail—made from materials from The Calamity itself. All that's left now is to load it into the cart and figure out how to use it."

"McCain the cart builder said he'd have a canopy added to the cart by this evening."

"Sounds like it'll be ready in time somehow or other, then. Now I suppose you'd better give the weapon a shot and make sure it'll do the job against the Simian Lord."

"Yeah, I was just thinking so myself. Can I get your help with that, Madoka?"

"I'm mentally ready whenever you are!" Madoka said as she bowed, but I knew that she had to be nervous at the prospect of playing a major role in our fight with the Simian Lord. "...I'm so glad to have a chance to fight with you. I guess I must be trembling with excitement..."

"That must be it. I'll admit I'm nervous, too—but don't worry, Madoka. I'll do whatever it takes to make sure you stay out of harm's way."

You never know how a battle is going to go until you've actually fought it. Adding vague words on top of that uncertainty would only serve to make my party even less confident.

"Atobe, you're taking on way too much by yourself. Remember, we're all with you."

"Igarashi..."

"It feels strange for me to be the one saying this...but Arihito, don't try to do it all yourself," said Elitia. "If anything happens to any of our allies, we'll be there to help for sure. If we can't manage that much, then we won't be able to help Rury or any of the other Seekers under the Simian Lord's control, either."

Other Seekers hadn't even managed to defeat the Simian Lord's monster underlings. Everyone had made it a point to keep their distance, thinking it wasn't worth the risk. Not only were we going up against a monster like that, but we'd given ourselves a difficult stipulation that we'd have to stick to during the fight.

"You and the rest of the party have surprised me many times over already. It probably sounds a little naive, but I believe you'll surprise me again."

"...I think so myself," I told Elitia. "We've got to push onward without hesitation, or it won't amount to anything. That's how we've done things so far."

"You got that right," Ceres agreed. "I don't know about you, but I've never heard of any Seekers in the history of the Labyrinth Country who've progressed as fast as your party... I don't figure it's much of an exaggeration at this point to say you've set a speed record. Wouldn't want this to trip you up, now would we?"

"*Mr. Atobe, I... No, now is not the time. Perhaps you'll let me finish that thought when your battle is won.*"

"Careful, Steiner—you'll jinx us," said Misaki. "But maybe I'm to blame, not treating all this with the seriousness it deserves..."

What could Steiner have wanted to talk to me about? I could've ventured a guess, but it would've been wrong to bring it up then and there.

"So when are you heading into the Blazing Red Mansion?" Ceres asked me.

"The hex on Theresia has progressed to the point that I'd rather not wait another day if we can help it. I underestimated it... I didn't even consider that it might get worse as Theresia defeated monsters."

"There are all sorts of ways for a hex to progress... That's nothing you should blame yourself over, Arihito. It was my oversight, too," Lynée said, cutting into the conversation. But she hadn't made any oversight at all—on the contrary, without her help, we couldn't have arrived at a way to break the hex.

"Hmm...? Ceres, what's this armor over here?"

"That? Arihito's party found that plate mail in a Black Box. It hasn't been appraised yet, so it can't be equipped."

"*You wouldn't happen to have a High-Grade Appraisal Scroll, would you, Ms. Lynée?*"

Steiner showed a great deal of respect toward Lynée—perhaps because she and Ceres had been childhood friends. Lynée, looking tickled by Steiner's respectful manner, opened the bag slung from her shoulder and began rummaging around inside it.

"I thought this might come in handy someday, though I've been holding on to it for quite a while. High-Grade Appraisal... Now, this scroll happens to be above even an Appraise 3 skill, so it's worth as much as a rare treasure itself. Indeed, it was once a treasure in my eyes."

Once—meaning it no longer was. While I mulled that over, Lynée burst out laughing, as if she'd read my innermost thoughts.

"To Schwarz and me, you and your party practically shine these days. I was delighted when you came out to my humble abode. After I received Ceres's letter, I waffled back and forth over whether I should come see her or not, right up until the moment I arrived... But I'm glad that I did."

"...Shouldn't you be saying that to *me*?" Ceres grumbled quietly.

At that, Lynée laughed even harder, to the point that her shoulders shook. Then she passed me the scroll she'd drawn out of her bag.

"Thank you, Lynée. I'll put this to good use."

"Can I get started with the appraisal right away, Arihito?"

"Please do!"

Madoka moved over toward the pedestal that held the unidentified plate mail and opened the scroll. When she did, the armor—which had been dark and dull up until that moment—began to give off a bright light.

◆★Glacial Plate◆
> Primarily made of crystium

> Refitted for extensive weight reduction
> Strengthens physical defense
> Slightly strengthens indirect defense
> Strengthens magic defense
> Nullifies area effect: High Heat
> Occasionally activates ICE SHIELD when
  taking damage from enemies
> One slot
> Currently broken

"...I'm starting to feel cooler just being near this armor..."

Madoka was surprised, and she wasn't the only one; Appraisal Scrolls and skills provided unknown details about things, but somehow this High-Grade Appraisal Scroll seemed different.

"Items that call for more than Appraise 3 have certain information concealed, so not just anybody can use them," Ceres explained. "Now that it's been appraised, you're getting a look at its true form."

"Chilly armor...and starred, on top of that. And it even has a slot, which means it can take a rune," Lynée added.

"It says it's broken, but really, it just looks like the clasps are busted. We could easily fix that with the proper materials... Though that's assuming we can get some crystium..."

"I think we found some of that metal in the last labyrinth we visited," Melissa said, reaching into her pockets. Sure enough, she pulled out the crystium fragments. Seeing them, Steiner gave a thumbs-up.

"I can have the armor fixed in two hours. Should I alter it to fit Seraphina, like my Master suggested?"

"Are you sure it's all right for me to take such powerful armor?"

"Sure," I said. "I was going to ask them to repair the armor you've been wearing so far, too. Can you do that, too, Steiner?"

"Ah… It looks like this armor is badly damaged indeed. It's going to take quite some time to fix. Could you let me think about how to properly restore it later?"

"Please do. You can repair and alter this Glacial Plate now, though, right?"

"Of course. I'll get it sized just right. You'll have to let me borrow Seraphina for a bit, Mr. Atobe."

With that, Steiner led Seraphina into the back area of the workshop with the Glacial Plate in hand.

"We'll also perform maintenance on the rest of your equipment. I'll see to all of it before tomorrow morning."

"Thanks, Ceres."

"In that case, I may as well stick around and lend a hand. I wouldn't want to head back now and have everyone think I'm heartless," said Lynée.

"If that's your reason for helping, you needn't bother."

If Ceres's words hurt Lynée's feelings, she didn't show any sign of it. They seemed less like childhood friends and more like sisters; if anything, this bickering felt like proof of the affection they shared for each other.

"…Hmph. Arihito, one of the magic stones on your slingshot is split," Ceres noted.

"It looks like I used that manipulation stone past its limit. If possible, I'd like to temporarily swap it out for another stone..."

"All right, then. How about if I take the Satisfaction Stone out of that Bloodsucker you showed me before and put that in your slingshot?"

According to Madoka's research, either Melissa or Theresia could use Bloodsucker. However, Melissa already had her butcher's knife and Forbidden Scythe, and Theresia had the Gloria Stiletto and Elluminate Razor Sword, so there was nobody to wield Bloodsucker at the moment.

"Bloodsucker belongs to Shirone, so it'd be best to return it to its original condition before we give it back to her... But the Gloria Stiletto presents something of an exceptional case, so we'll just have to explain the next time we see her."

"Right... That settles it, then. We'll borrow the Satisfaction Stone. As for the Silent Stone on the Gloria Stiletto, we'll move that over to Suzuna's flute."

"If an enemy tries to cast a spell or something, Silence can probably prevent it... Is that it?"

Silence seemed like it would be useful for neutralizing the Seekers that the Simian Lord had under its control. As long as we could afflict them with that status ailment, it wouldn't matter how mercilessly they attacked; any skills that called for chanting would be unusable.

"Should I add a spot for another magic stone on the flute, then? I'd have to use another pinch of Sterling Silver Sand."

"Yes, please."

"Typically we can't add another slot for magic stones unless we can also guarantee that it won't lead to a decrease in power, but that shouldn't be a problem for the flute."

◆Processed Equipment◆
> ★GLACIAL PLATE was repaired using CRYSTIUM FRAGMENT
> ★GLACIAL PLATE was equipped with ALTER RUNE Became ★ALTERED GLACIAL PLATE
> ★PAN'S ECHO +1 was altered with STERLING SILVER SAND ⟶ Number of equippable magic stones increased by 1
> ★PAN'S ECHO +1 was equipped with SILENT STONE ⟶ Upgraded to +2
> BLACK MAGICAL SLINGSHOT +3 was equipped with SATISFACTION STONE ⟶ Upgraded to +4

We couldn't be sure where the exact effects of these upgrades would be seen. Still, anything that gave us even just one more tactical option would certainly prove its worth if we were backed into a corner.

"Sorry to trouble you while you're busy, Mr. Atobe, but if I may ask for your Seekers' report…"

Louisa had just arrived, having finished up her work at the guild. I had to tell her, too, that we'd be heading into the Blazing Red Mansion the next day. As calmly as I could manage, I filled her in on the situation and also asked her to check whether we'd qualified to enter five-star labyrinths yet.

Part III: The Prebattle Meeting; Lynée's Past

Back in the living room of our quarters at the inn, I showed Louisa my license. She checked its display with her monocle, then looked up with a smile.

◆Expedition Results◆
> Raided 1F through 3F of Trembling Foothills: 30 points
> Raided uncharted area of Trembling Foothills: 100 points
> Discovered unexplored territory in Trembling Foothills: 2,000 points
> Kyouka grew to level 8: 80 points
> Suzuna grew to level 7: 70 points
> Misaki grew to level 7: 70 points
> Cion grew to level 8: 80 points
> Became friendly with ★Stray Strada: 420 points
> Defeated 1 Deep Eater: 120 points
> Party members' Trust Levels increased: 240 points
Seeker Contribution: 3,210 points
District Five Provisional Contribution Ranking: 288

"Congratulations, Mr. Atobe! You're now approved to go seeking in five-star labyrinths!"

"Thanks, Louisa. I had no idea that discovering unexplored territory would raise our contribution score that much…"

"It's worth so many points, there are some Seekers who actually specialize in finding unexplored territory. The Guild itself goes to great lengths to stay abreast of such areas; that way, we can more easily dispatch rescue teams to help Seekers who might run into trouble looking for them. Of course, to get those contribution points, Seekers have to come back safely, and their licenses have to acknowledge the region as unexplored territory, too."

"If we hadn't run into this monster called the Strada, we wouldn't have discovered the unexplored territory in the first place. I think we'd better be ready to look at whatever happens in labyrinths from a different angle from now on."

"I—I suppose so… I'm sorry, Mr. Atobe. I may have taken it in stride at first, but the truth is I've never seen something like this line item about befriending the Strada before. That is, I've seen plenty of items for defeating monsters, and for taming monsters, but… Again, I'm sorry. I'm embarrassed to see that there are license line items that I'm not familiar with, given my position."

"I guess there are monsters out there who can communicate… But we didn't know any more about that than you did. With high-enough levels, we might even be able to recruit them."

I had no idea whether we'd ever meet the Strada again or not. All of this was something to consider after we'd beaten the Simian Lord.

Yukari had said that things really began at District Seven,

but my party and I couldn't move on to our next phase until we'd finally beaten the foe that we'd been after for such a long time.

"…You're all ready to go tomorrow, then."

"Right. We'll defeat the Simian Lord and come back to tell the tale."

Louisa gave me a look. She couldn't hide the uncertainty on her face; her concern conveyed her kindness more than anything else could have.

"Please allow me to shake your hand like this again as soon as you're back. There is much that I want to tell you, Mr. Atobe… much that I want to say."

"Me too, Louisa… Wait, what's wrong?"

Louisa was laughing, seeming to be at a complete loss. Her cheeks looked a bit red, but that might have just been my imagination.

"…Please be sure to return safely to file your next Seekers' report with me. I eagerly await it."

It seemed she might've been trying to say something else, but at the time, I didn't realize it.

I would definitely be back to hear Louisa out. Since I'd arrived in the Labyrinth Country, I'd come to want to know more about other people than I had before.

"We should grab a drink again sometime, too. Some things you just can't say any other way."

"Certainly, Mr. Atobe. If that's what you wish, I'd be delighted to fill your cup."

This was a tough one...but I was grateful that we could speak to each other like this. I thought about that as I watched Louisa rise from her chair and leave.

One by one, my party members who'd leveled up came to see me and confirm their skills. Igarashi was the first to arrive. She sat down on the sofa opposite from me and showed me her license.

"Do you think this means those of us who were level six or seven received extra experience points?"

"I'm pretty sure all it means is that everyone really put forth their best efforts. It looks like I'm starting to get close to my next level up, too..."

"Levels can increase even inside labyrinths, right?"

"Right, they can. For the most part, people only check and see that they've gained a level after they leave the labyrinth, but they increase while you're seeking. You can only gain up to one level on each excursion, though."

"In that case, it should be possible to gain another level in another fight before we face the Simian Lord."

"If that happens, we'll have a last-minute chance to acquire new skills...but there's too much uncertainty to consider it a sure thing. We should just keep in mind that it's a possibility and not bet on it."

"That makes sense."

◆New Available Skills — Kʏᴏᴜᴋᴀ◆
Level 3 Skills
Divinity: Grants a target Saint's Breath,
    giving any humanoid enemies that
    attack them the Enlightened status.
    (Prerequisite: Einherjar)

Level 2 Skills
Thunder Strike: Attacks one enemy with
    bolts of lightning. Strikes between 1 and
    8 times. The target cannot be chosen.
    (Prerequisite: Thunderbolt)
Warrior Procession: Lessens the effects
    of disadvantageous terrain on the user's
    party.

Remaining Skill Points: 4

Perhaps because she'd grown in level so much, there were no new level-1 skills available on the list.

"What do you think this Enlightened status means, Atobe? In Japanese, that would be pronounced *kyouka*, but...I mean, I'm sure it's a coincidence."

Igarashi looked a little embarrassed as she added that last part. It did indeed sound a lot like her given name, and I guess that concerned her.

"There's a detailed explanation here. It looks like it's a status ailment that makes an enemy attack less frequently for the duration of the fight...but conditions have to be met for it to work."

"It lowers their attack frequency... That sounds useful, but it takes getting hit once to work in the first place. Combining it with Mirage Step would lower the risk, but with Einherjar as a prerequisite, there's not enough points left over for that."

"In that case, maybe you'd better choose from skills you've passed up before."

"Right... Perhaps it'd be best to take Dance of the Warrior Maiden 1 and Pole Dance. Assuming the Charm status ailment gets through to them, that might stop the subordinated Seekers from attacking."

At first, I wasn't too sure about Igarashi making use of both of those skills, but I realized she was right: If that combination worked properly, it would be particularly effective on the male Seekers the Simian Lord had dominated.

"The only question is whether that'll work on an opponent under the Simian Lord's control... Thunder Strike is powerful, and I bet there'll be a use for Earth Puppet and Freezing Thorns, too."

"True...but Earth Puppet seems to depend on my own strength, so even if we use it to make a decoy, it won't last for very long. And Freezing Thorns might slow our enemies down, but it can't stop them completely. Think I should stick to a combination of skills that has a chance of totally shutting enemies down, don't you?"

"Good point... All right, then. Dance of the Warrior Maiden 1 and Pole Dance it is."

"With just a few more skill points, I could give Einherjar a try...but the likelihood of that working on an opponent over my own level is low."

Einherjar is a skill that allows its user to turn immobilized enemies into allies, but its success rate depends on the difference in ability between its user and its target. With that in mind, Pole Dance—which would raise Igarashi's agility and evasion rate and allow her to charm enemies—seemed like the more realistically effective option.

"Just one point left... If it could exploit the Simian Lord's weaknesses, Freezing Weapon would be a good choice, but all we really know about it is that it's a fire elemental monster."

"Right...and considering that it's mostly going to be level-two skills and up appearing on the list from now on, we should probably hang on to spare points to acquire skills when we really need them."

"In other words, this is a process we have to go through—not the destination itself."

Igarashi was exactly right. Still, even level-1 skills could really come in handy in times of need. As long as we picked the skills we needed when we needed them, they wouldn't go to waste.

"Maybe I should use Ambivalenz tomorrow..."

"I think we should save that for when we really need it. The weaker you are, the stronger it gets...and it also inflicts damage on us. It's an extremely dangerous weapon."

"...You're right, Atobe. I'll only break it out when it's absolutely necessary. I'll send the next person in to see you."

"Tell you what—would you send Misaki and Suzuna in together?"

"Sure. Just a moment."

With that, Igarashi stood up. She looked behind me, toward the spot where Theresia usually stood—but she wasn't there. Kozelka was staying at the same inn as us tonight, and Theresia was with her. We'd discussed having her bring Theresia here once these skill selection meetings were over so I could see how she was doing.

"Heya, Arihito! Holding up okay?"

"Are you sure Misaki and I can come in together?"

"Yeah. I'm thinking the two of you should work together this time, so I called you in as a pair."

I started off with a look at Misaki's license. All the new skills added to her list were exactly the sort of things you'd expect for a Gambler like her.

```
◆New Available Skills — MISAKI◆
Level 3 Skills
Luck Balance: As failed actions accumulate,
    this skill increases the likelihood that
    further actions will succeed. Activation
    period resets with each new day. Target is
    limited to one party member.


Level 2 Skills
Machine Gun Shuffle: Throws card-type
```

weapons in rapid succession for repeated
attacks. The more cards are thrown, the
more damage is inflicted. (Prerequisite:
Double Draw)
Russian Roulette 2: Chooses a random target
and sets their luck to "disastrous."
(Prerequisite: Russian Roulette 1)

Level 1 Skills
Risky Raise: Boosts both an enemy's stats
and the amount of experience points earned
by defeating them.

Remaining Skill Points: 5

"Ooh, a level-three skill showed up on my list! It doesn't really look like it'd be useful right away, though... Still, I bet it'd pack a punch in the back half of a really long mission."

"'As failed actions accumulate,' huh...? In that case, maybe we could have a few low-cost skills fizzle on purpose before setting out into the labyrinth... I dunno, it'd be risky to try."

"Yeah... Feels like there's some real cheaty potential there, though. Russian Roulette 2 giving someone 'disastrous' luck sounds pretty astounding, but if it picks one of us at random instead of a monster, that could be really bad news... And I don't have enough cards to use Machine Gun Shuffle."

"Let me guess, Misaki. You're planning on picking Pool Cap, aren't you?"

"Ah-ha-ha... Does it show? Yep, that's exactly what I'm gonna do. I don't think I'll get too much use out of it, but having it could make a really big difference."

If a member of our party took a fatal attack, Pool Cap could reduce the damage just enough to keep them in the fight. However, Misaki would end up taking half of the amount of damage that it reduced herself. It's a skill meant to be used when an ally is in a really tight spot. If only there were some way to prevent it from putting Misaki at such great risk... Ideally, there'd be an option to reroute that damage over to me. That would be great.

"How 'bout this? I'll spend two points to pick up Pool Cap and save the rest for when they'll be useful! 'Course, it's pretty hard to keep track of what skills I could potentially learn..."

"Misaki...," said Suzuna.

"Aw, c'mon, don't get all serious on me! I know using Pool Cap is dangerous and the best thing is to just win without it," Misaki said, slapping Suzuna on the shoulder.

Suzuna kept her concerned comments to herself, but I could tell that she really wanted to say something to dissuade Misaki.

"All right, Suzuna's up next! Time for me to zip my lips and watch!"

◆New Available Skills — SUZUNA◆
Level 3 Skills
Sacred Song: The user accepts a spirit into
     their body, allowing them to temporarily

gain that spirit's abilities. Requires
a musical instrument. (Prerequisites:
Medium, Resonant Sound)

Level 2 Skills
Anoint: Sprinkles party members with
    purifying water, distributing damage from
    enemy elemental attacks and reducing the
    amount of damage incurred in proportion
    to the number of people anointed. Works
    one time only. (Prerequisites: Handwash,
    Purification)

Remaining Skill Points: 3

"Sacred Song and Anoint..."

"When it says 'a spirit,' do you think that might include Ariadne?"

Before I could answer Suzuna's question, I heard Ariadne's voice echoing in my head.

"I believe I would be a potential target. But if a Seeker who had made no pact with me used the same skill, I do not believe I could inhabit them. I cannot deny the possibility that a strange Seeker could use a different skill to summon me, but it remains to be seen for certain."

"Thanks, Ariadne. Supposing you could use your own power while inside Suzuna, what would happen?"

"I could act to keep the Shrine Maiden out of harm's way.

However, with my parts aligned, my strength differs from when I am moving on my own; there are limits to the skills that I may employ."

"Huh? You mean Suzuna and Ariadne can, like, *combine*? That's gotta be superstrong..."

"*My skills do not provide exceptional attack power. They all depend on my parts.*"

Even so, if it meant we could draw on Ariadne's power in a different way than we had been thus far, it was certain to be a big help.

"Okay, then... Shall I take Sacred Song?"

"Yeah, let's go with that."

Suzuna used her license to acquire the Sacred Song skill. As I'd expect of a level-3 skill, it had multiple prerequisites—and power to match the price.

Cion had also leveled up, but since she was a guard dog, I couldn't choose skills for her from my license. Her skills had already been acquired, and I'd just have to find out what they were in actual combat.

"Haaah... That moment when you pick a new skill sure gets your heart pounding, huh?"

"Yeah... Every single time, I always wonder whether I'm making the right choice, or whether something else would be better. But they're decisions we've got to make if we're going to move forward."

"I'll do my best to think about when each skill would be most useful. Please rest well, Arihito... Good night."

"'Night, Arihito!"

And with that, Suzuna and Misaki stood and left the room. They might have said good night, but sleep was the last thing on my mind. Even as we'd sat there considering skills, the hex had kept eating away at Theresia. Our average level was still lower than it should have been, and it was hard to say we were properly prepared for what we would face the next day.

We've finally come this far...and yet, somewhere in my heart, I'm afraid of what tomorrow will bring.

"You look like something's on your mind, Arihito," a voice said to me out of the blue. Ceres was standing right there in the room with me—though I could have sworn she hadn't been there before.

"C-Ceres... I'm sorry—I didn't notice you were there."

"Good. I came in quietly so you wouldn't. It looks like you and your party are finished with your meetings."

"We are. I'm still not entirely sure which skills will be most effective, but at least we put a lot of thought into picking them."

"What is a skill point, anyway, hmm? Some say they're the measure of a Seeker's potential. You could say Seekers borrow power from their licenses to *choose* that potential."

"Potential... That makes sense. I think you've hit the nail on the head, Ceres."

"Me? I don't know any more than you do. We jades may have been in the Labyrinth Country long before you, but talking to you never fails to surprise me, Arihito. I expect it's beyond me to know everything there is to know about this place."

Ceres set a glass of water down in front of me and sat down on the sofa facing slightly toward me.

"I hoped to talk a bit...about Lynée," she said.

"I'm glad to listen to anything you don't mind me hearing. I'm not exactly in the mood to sleep just yet, anyway."

"Okay, then, I'll take you up on that. Once I'm done blabbing, I might even set you up with a little sleep magic."

Ceres spoke in such a calm way that I started feeling calmer myself just listening to her. Something about her that evening was a little different from how she usually carried herself in front of Steiner.

"Long ago, Lynée lived in the same place I did. She became a Seeker before me, mind you. She moved up to District Five, while I hit my limits in District Six and left the seeking life. I'm sure you can imagine why I was in District Eight when you met me. After I put some distance between myself and seeking and went to live on my own, tossing the rest of the world aside, my contribution points started on a constant decline. The very picture of frustration and failure, isn't it?"

"But you still met Steiner and started up your workshop..."

"Sure did. I met Steiner... Well, there's no reason to keep up the 'walking suit of armor' charade, is there? I met Chiara when she was a tiny little thing and practically raised her like my own daughter. She can do more than just blacksmithing; she's got the skills to make armor that I built move like it's alive. That's how she controls that armor, even though it's so much bigger than she is."

"I had no idea..."

I had wondered why Chiara had taken on the name Steiner and stayed inside that huge suit of armor. I'd figured her reasons would stay a mystery to me forever. And yet here Ceres was, explaining it to me.

"That scarecrow Lynée keeps with her... That's an old partner of hers she lost to a monster in a labyrinth. Or at least her attempt at a magical restoration."

"...!"

I was at a loss for words. Schwarz, who'd guided us before, was a former Seeker...and what's more, one who had died on the job.

"Lynée ran into the Altargeist—not in the Twilight Lakeside Stroll, but in another labyrinth. Unfortunately for Lynée, her party was struck with a status ailment that caused allies to attack each other. She still can't talk about what happened after that."

At last, I realized why Lynée had set up her hermitage inside a labyrinth. I imagined she'd heard word that the Altargeist had reappeared and wanted to be ready to take its revenge. If it was a different labyrinth, though, it might not be the same monster— still, Lynée had to capture the Altargeist.

"You know, Lynée was very grateful to you, Arihito. That eccentric old bat even says she's never seen a Rearguard with as much guts as you've got."

"I'm the one who should be grateful to her. I was going to pay another visit to that labyrinth myself."

"The more time passes by, the less time we'll have with Theresia still calm. You've got to get that hex the Simian Lord put on her cleared up as soon as possible."

"I agree. That's why we're definitely taking down the Simian Lord tomorrow."

"...Hmph. I know it may be naive for me to tell a grown man like you anything that'll get your hopes up, but here goes. I believe in you."

Ceres hadn't just come to tell me about Lynée; she'd also come to cheer me on.

"Now, like I told you before, you'd better give the Queen's Tail a test run to make sure it's got the power you need. While you're at it, you might find some ways to use it that you hadn't thought of before, too."

"Thanks, I plan on it. How long does it take before we can fire it again after using it?"

"Thirty minutes at most, so be sure to pick your shots carefully. I did rig it with a mechanism that charges it up with magic power all on its own, but with an external supply of dynamic power, it'll go quicker."

In that case, my skills would come in handy. If I could use Charge Assist on a weapon, I might be able to come up with a way to get the Queen's Tail ready to fire again in less time.

"Now then. Back to the workshop with me. I've still got finishing touches to apply."

"I'm sorry for keeping you so late, Ceres... Please try to get some rest between now and the morning."

Ceres gave me a smile and a nod as she left the room. I heard her speaking briefly from outside, like she'd passed somebody in the hallway.

My next visitor of the evening was Kozelka—and Theresia arrived with her.

"Theresia said she wanted to come here, so I brought her over."

"Thanks for that, Kozelka."

"…Just think of it as if I'm here to stand guard for you. That's all."

With that, Kozelka bowed and stepped back out of the room. She'd pulled a few strings so that she was here on official business keeping watch over us, all so Theresia could be with me again. In fact, she had no intention of staying in the room with me and Theresia.

Kozelka, who always solemnly followed regulations, had accommodated Theresia and me at her own personal discretion. I knew this wasn't a debt I could easily repay.

"……"

Without a word, Theresia looked at me. She moved over toward the magic item that filled the room with light, then shot a look back in my direction.

"Ah, you can go ahead and turn that out. It's about time we got some rest."

Theresia nodded and turned out the light. But even though the room was dark, she didn't go to lie down on the sofa. She just remained standing.

"…Somehow this feels like back when we first met. You never slept. You just watched me the whole time…"

"......"

It wasn't the moment for reminiscing, but seeing Theresia as she was, I couldn't help but see how the present overlapped with the past.

Theresia didn't lie down on the sofa; all she did was watch me. Leila had once said that there was no proof that demi-humans have emotions. Maybe Theresia was the exception, rather than the rule...but that felt foolish. Still, the more my mind lingered on how Theresia was keeping her distance, and why she wasn't even trying to sleep, the harder I found it to even breathe.

"......"

"...Theresia."

Theresia walked over to me. She reached out and touched my shoulder, then pulled her hand back again.

"I get it. This can't go well if I'm on edge."

"......"

Theresia shook her head slightly. A moment later, she nodded.

I wanted so badly to hear her voice, to know what she was thinking and what that gesture had meant—

I put a lid on those desires and lay down on the couch. All I wanted to do was close my eyes.

The only light in the room was weak and dim—essentially a nightlight to prevent total darkness. Theresia's watchful shape seemed to float through the dark room like a phantom, drifting in and out of my vision.

No. She was no phantom. I'd get her back. Theresia and Elitia's friend Rury—I'd get them both back.

Part IV: True Intentions

That night, I had a longer and more vivid dream than usual.

I was back working in my office from before I came to the Labyrinth Country. A coworker—who was trying to get me to come along on the company ski trip—came by to ask how my work was going, and I told him I was making decent progress, even though in truth I was excruciatingly busy.

The day-to-day grind of my old job wasn't without its little joys. When work I submitted earned me some praise, for instance, or when the presentation that Igarashi and I had put together was enough of a success to earn us an award.

I didn't spare many moments to think about life or death. I did every now and then, but the thoughts were always fleeting.

It was a peaceful life—and it was no mistake for me to take that peace for granted. Even though I'd grown used to life as a Seeker in the Labyrinth Country, I still didn't think it was wrong to assume those peaceful days would last.

But despite all that, I never wanted to go back.

We were headed for a destination that was unclear. But still, there was something I had to see through to the end in the Labyrinth Country.

When I met Theresia, I found what I was meant to do as a Rearguard.

Demi-humans were supposedly emotionless and put to work as mercenaries. When I heard about lizardmen, I pictured exactly what the word makes them sound like: some kind of bipedal reptile-human hybrid. I wonder what I would've thought if that had been who I'd met at the Mercenary Office.

But it wasn't. It was Theresia. A girl who'd already died in a labyrinth once before. When I first heard about that bit of personal history, I didn't think too deeply about it. I figured it must be something that happens pretty often in the Labyrinth Country.

Was Theresia emotionless? Of course not. That might have been exceptional among demi-humans, but I'd caught a glimpse of emotion from Ferris as well—and I know her family understood it, too.

Even so, I caught myself thinking, somewhere deep inside, that Theresia wasn't a normal human being, either.

As a demi-human, she didn't feel any embarrassment at the prospect of taking a bath with someone else. Actually, even if she was told not to do so, she still wanted to. I chalked that up to her being a demi-human, too.

…Maybe she was only so faithful to me because she was a demi-human.

If that was really the case, then I wouldn't be able to forgive myself for taking advantage of her demi-humanity. I wanted to make her human again. Then I would see if it was true or not and confront my own ego.

If only Theresia could speak… If only I could understand more of what she thought…

Only then would I be able to face her without feeling some sort of inferiority complex.

There was probably more that she wanted to do than just constantly go seeking with me. But she might have felt she had no choice but to go along with whatever plan I laid out for her. I really hoped that wasn't true.

I hoped that we'd reach the cathedral in District Four, but at the same time, I was afraid to go. Part of me thought the Simian Lord's hex was a punishment for my uncertainty. Theresia put aside all fear and played her role as best she could for the good of our party—so why couldn't I give her my complete and total trust?

I had no way of knowing whether Theresia would want to keep traveling with me if she ever became human again.

Even the fact that she'd attacked me felt like a sort of payback. Part of me wanted her to blame me. Even if nobody around me had actually touched on it, it was there, like an open wound.

The total arrogance of hoping for perfection—even though I knew it would be impossible to push forward without anyone getting hurt or taking any risks.

"...*Master*..."

In my dream, I heard a voice. It dragged my consciousness up from the depths of darkness.

It was Murakumo's voice. I'm pretty sure it was trying to warn me of something.

I slightly opened my eyes. There, in the darkened room, I saw

Theresia lying beside me, peering over me. Her hands were totally empty, but she had them at my neck. She wasn't squeezing, though; her hands simply stayed on my neck without any force being applied.

I knew exactly what had happened. Still, I didn't check my license.

"I...I..."

I didn't mind dying if Theresia was the one doing the killing. But that thought was only a cheap escape.

Theresia's hands were cool on my neck. As I felt her cold touch, something fell onto my cheek. A tear had fallen from Theresia's own cheek as she leaned over me. The unbroken trail it left behind on her face gleamed white in the darkness.

She'd removed the suit that she usually wore. In the dim light of the room, an even lighter paleness shone out through her white skin.

When Theresia started unclasping her suit in the bath, I'd looked away immediately. *Obviously*, I'd thought, *I mustn't look at her.* I felt guilt because I knew that if I looked directly at Theresia's body, I wouldn't be able to help feeling a surge of emotion.

Theresia had received a Slave Seal. That made it so much worse. *Taking a bath with her under those conditions in the first place was the wrong thing to do*, I thought; even just imagining it was wrong.

Demi-humans got hired as assassins. There were probably some people who didn't treat their demi-human mercenaries with respect. I thought I couldn't be one of those people. I never wanted to treat Theresia like that, and I definitely never would hurt her.

And yet look how things had turned out.

Theresia was crying. Maybe some demi-humans didn't have emotions, but I knew it—that didn't apply to her. She blamed herself for something. She took my hand and pulled it toward her.

I didn't resist.

But I knew that Theresia was trying to hurt herself, and I would absolutely not let that happen.

"……"

Theresia's pulse grew surprisingly fast. Either she was nervous, or she thought this wasn't really the right thing to do. Whichever it was, I couldn't just lie back and watch her.

I sat up and wrapped my arms around Theresia's back, holding her.

"……!"

"You're freezing cold… What are you trying to do, Theresia? …I guess you're not even trying to hide it. This is all really drastic."

Theresia didn't move. Her body was shivering. I loosened my hold on her a bit, and she showed signs of trying to squirm away.

"I'm not angry with you, Theresia," I assured her. "If I'm angry at anybody, it's myself. You've got so much on your mind, and I'm over here trying to gloss over it, like we can just march over there together tomorrow and fix everything."

"……"

I could tell Theresia everything that was on my mind, but the conversation would be one-sided since she couldn't speak. Our relationship felt totally out of balance. But still, I had to tell her—and I had to tell her now. If I didn't, there was no way I could calm her down.

"When I first stepped out into this world as a Seeker, I didn't know where I was going or what I was doing. What gave me sight of hope back then was meeting you, Theresia. It all started with you."

"……"

"You probably think I'm exaggerating, but it's true. I'm completely useless by myself. But thanks to you by my side, I've gotten more confident, little by little."

Theresia gave her head a little shake at first, but as I continued talking, she stopped.

There I was, a grown man, trembling just because I was saying what needed to be said. I knew that I'd feel pathetic when I looked back, but there was no getting away from it.

"Everyone in our party is younger than me... Some of them by a decade. This might be something I'm pushing on you against your will, but I've come to think of all of you—including you, Theresia—like you're my little sisters. Igarashi, Louisa, and Seraphina are closer to my age than the rest, but I still feel mostly the same way about them... The reason I came all this way to see you is because I thought that, if I broke a rule I set for myself, we wouldn't be able to stay together for long."

Theresia no longer showed any sign of trying to get away.

I let go of her and put a little space between us, still facing her. Then I reached up and wiped away the tracks that her tears had left behind on her cheek with my finger. She kept completely still.

"But really, I had to make sure of a few things. Whether we made a proper party together, whether you were people I should respect…and beyond that, how I was seeing all of you as members of the opposite sex."

"……"

Theresia sniffled as she listened. I realized she must be cold and draped my blanket over her shoulders.

She'd made no efforts to hide her pale, exposed skin until she was under the blanket. Then, finally, she pulled it in tight to cover herself.

"But seeing you that way, even a little bit, is against my rules. Truth be told, I've always thought that it wasn't really okay for us to be bathing together."

"……"

Theresia slightly lowered her eyes. If I had to guess where she was looking, I'd say she was looking at herself.

"W-wait, don't get me wrong… Listen, Theresia, I don't know if this is exactly what you think I mean, but it's not wrong because it's *you*. Truth be told, a small part of me is happy about it…and that's what makes it wrong."

"……"

Theresia was no longer crying. She looked in my direction with an ear toward me, as if to show me that she was listening.

I had never been completely sure how much of what I said got through to Theresia, no matter how many times I said it, but at last, I'd reached her loud and clear. All it took was telling her my true feelings—ones that I never would have expressed out loud under normal circumstances.

"I don't want you to blame yourself for attacking me, Theresia. I don't want you to do anything you don't want to do. That's absolutely not— Huh?"

Theresia was shaking her head all the way from side to side. I assumed that was in response to some part of what I'd been saying. Was it the part about not wanting her to do what she didn't want to? If so, what did the head shaking mean?

"……"

I wanted to leave it unmentioned; maybe act like I hadn't noticed because the room was too dark. But Theresia had gone red in a flash—both her lizard mask and the part of her actual face that was visible underneath it.

"……"

"I…I see… But seriously, I don't want you to…"

I'd assumed that Theresia felt so guilty about attacking me that she'd taken off her suit to make it up to me somehow. But it looked like that wasn't the case.

The next day, we'd be off to fight the Simian Lord. Before that, she wanted to… Well, whatever she intended to do, she'd ended up watching me as I slept. That was when the hex had kicked in and made her reach for my neck.

It's not that she didn't want it. But even so, it was good that I woke up when I did—even though it took Murakumo's warning for me to get my eyes open.

"Let's just take it easy and rest for tonight. I'll keep watch over you until you fall asleep."

"……"

Theresia looked a bit uncertain, but before too long, she nodded.

I thought she'd take the sofa diagonally across from mine—but instead, she sat right beside me and looked directly at me.

"...I guess it's a bit embarrassing to be watched when you're awake. Tell you what, let's share lookout responsibilities."

Theresia nodded. I lay my head down in her lap, and she started patting it.

"...Just for a bit, though. You need rest, too, Theresia..."

She nodded once again. I'm pretty sure that under her lizard mask, she was smiling.

Part V: Morning of the Decisive Battle

I woke up just as the sky started turning light.

Naturally, I didn't sleep the night away with my head on Theresia's lap. Once Theresia drifted off to sleep herself, I got down and left her to it. With her sharp senses, I thought she might notice, but it seemed that she slept extra-deeply. I managed to lay her down and drape a blanket over her without her so much as stirring.

◆Theresia's Status◆
▶ Evil Domination progression: 48

I had been optimistic to estimate that the hex wouldn't put her at risk until its progression hit 100. Even at its current value, I couldn't be sure of when Theresia might turn hostile toward us. Even with Lynée's skills helping stave off that danger, all we could do was hope that nothing would go wrong until we faced the Simian Lord in battle.

I'm pretty sure ten hours have passed since the last time I checked Theresia's status. It's only gone up by two progression points since then...

If the events of the previous night had affected the hex's progression somehow, that meant it didn't necessarily grow in a linear fashion; it might be possible to slow it down.

However, that wasn't certain—and none of this meant anything without a way to make it actually regress.

The day had come when we would defeat the Simian Lord and finally settle the score that our party had taken on when we met Elitia.

I washed the sleep out of my eyes and headed into the main room of our quarters. Just then, there was a light knock at our door.

"Just a moment… Ah, it's you, Luca."

"Good morning! I rented a room of my own to get some shut-eye—the beds in this inn are to die for, don't you think?"

Luca set a large leather trunk down in front of me. It was worn with years of use.

"I just so happen to have the suit you ordered ready to go… See? Wanna try it on?"

"Yes—but can I have a few moments to get ready first?"

"Sure. But don't forget to put on a real fighting man's face while you're at it, Arihito! Why, you're looking even more sweet and kind than usual right now. Come on, show me an expression that says, 'I'm a winner!'"

"Uh…I don't think that's going to happen."

With that, Luca stepped back out of the entrance to our suite. It seemed that when it came time to change, I'd be doing it in the room Luca was renting.

"Fwooo… What's that in the air? The scent of two grown-up men coming to a manly understanding…? Y'know, Ari-poo, the manly-man vibe really suits you!"

"It's kind of…um, 'hard-boiled,' maybe…? M-maybe not?"

"Oh, so you're into it, Suzu? You never really seem like you're all that into boys, so I wasn't sure."

"…Th-that's not it… I'm sorry, Arihito… You know how Misaki is…"

"You two are awake, too, huh? I'm afraid I've got to step out for a bit. Could you keep an eye on Theresia while she's resting in the living room?"

"O-okay…"

"Sure thing!"

Misaki and Suzuna must have heard Luca and me talking; they stepped out of the bedroom, still in their pajamas. Igarashi was right behind them, although she still looked pretty sleepy. I had to look away before I took in any more of her in her just-awakened state.

"Zzznh… Oh, Ari—I mean…Atobe!"

"G-good morning, Igarashi. Excuse me, I need to go wash my face."

"Sure. But you look fine as you are, too, you know. I like a little bit of scruff."

"…U-um, maybe you should get some more sleep, Kyouka."

"Nah…"

Maybe it was because she was still drowsy, but I got the feeling that Igarashi was saying things that she'd typically never say. Or it could be that there was just something wrong with my hearing.

"I…," Suzuna started. "I also think Arihito looks nice when he's just woken up."

"Y-yeah… Huh?" said Misaki.

I'd just stepped out of bed, looking dreary and disheveled, and here they were praising me for it. How was I supposed to take that? …No, that was a conundrum for another time.

Suzuna and Misaki retreated to their bedroom for a while, but I knew everyone would be ready to go by the time breakfast was done. I went back over to the sink and made another attempt at waking myself up with a splash of cold water.

I went by Luca's room and put on my new, freshly tailored suit. It was light and very breathable—clearly made from an entirely different material from typical suits.

"It looks like I got your size just right—I don't need to hem it or anything."

"It really is a perfect fit."

"I wrung out every last drop of my personal know-how to make this a killer combat suit. You do realize that you're basically the only Seeker who wears a suit into labyrinths, don't you, Arihito?"

"I gather they've even started calling me the Suit Guy, thanks to your tailoring."

To be honest, it probably had more to do with the fact that there wasn't much to distinguish me by, so people had to go with what they could see. Luca's shoulders shook as he laughed. Then he measured the length of the sleeves one last time and brushed off my back.

```
◆[MP] Black & White◆
 > Strengthens physical defense
 > Strengthens indirect defense
```

> Strengthens magic defense
> Slightly strengthens agility
> Slightly strengthens lightning attacks
> Devil Protection: Reduces damage from
  devil-type monster attacks
> Adds Lightning Resistance 1
> Adds Darkness Resistance 1
> Quality: Masterpiece
> Crafted by LUCA

"The fabrics are made with hair from two monsters: Darkness Blitz for the outside and Thunder Head for the lining. Hence the name Black & White. There are other components, too, but it seems the combination of those two monsters is what gives it that extra dash of resistance to devils. Armor needs to be a masterpiece or higher to add optional skills, but I'd say I've managed this time."

"Managed? It's amazing. It feels durable, but it's still easy to move around in."

"That's music to my ears. I'll get your old suit patched up, too, of course, but personally, I'd rather see you in a line of new suits even better than this one going forward... If you can get me the materials, that is."

"Sure thing. If we find anything that looks like you could use it, I'd love to discuss it with you. For now, I think this suit will do the trick, though."

Luca grinned so broadly, his eyes practically squeezed shut.

Then he turned to the holster, which I'd removed to try on the suit, and gave it a once over.

"It looks like you've been slinging a magic gun. Have you had to put it to work?"

"It's come in handy a few times already. It's a good match for my skills, and it's pretty versatile when it comes to tactics—with the right magic stones loaded, at least."

"...I knew it. You're a real *wolf*, through and through. You've got the snout for sniffing out a path to victory for you and your friends. Weren't you just bored to *death* doing office work in a more peaceful world?"

I supposed Luca had taken a guess at what my old job had been like, based on my penchant for suits. Maybe because he'd hit the bull's-eye, or maybe because the dream I'd had was still fresh in my mind, I gave him a straight answer.

"There were times when my old job felt fulfilling. But you're right, Luca. I don't think I really knew how it felt to be alive until I came to the Labyrinth Country. I guess that might sound a little ironic, considering how I got here."

"Hee-hee... A little. But—and this might make you laugh to even imagine—but I have a feeling that if we'd met before we were reborn, we'd still have been friends."

"You know...something about that feels really good to hear."

"You've got a gift for opening all kinds of people's eyes, Ari-hito. So get out there and live a little more selfishly!"

I'd always told people not to worry about me, that however

things ended up for me was okay. It was something of a foundational idea for me. I saw how that might sometimes make it seem like I didn't care if I threw my life away, though.

Still, I didn't just want to live; I wanted everyone else alive with me. That's why I tried to find any way I could out of a helpless situation. I didn't want to die; I was attached to life.

"...That wound on your chest has healed up. It looks like you were about one step away from kicking the bucket."

"You could say that... It doesn't hurt, though. Actually, it feels like proof that I'm ready."

I'd only blurted out exactly what I was thinking, but Luca stared at me in wonder. Or maybe I was freaking him out.

"The people who make it to the top are the ones who keep smiling, even when they're backed into a corner...or at least that's my theory. I'd like to see you grinning your way through a battle someday, Arihito."

"I'm not crazy about fighting, really," I said. "I only fight if that's what it takes to move onward."

Luca stuck out his fist, and I lightly bumped it with my own. With that, the two of us left the room and headed for the inn's entrance hall, where our fully equipped allies were waiting.

Madoka had arranged for our cart to be brought over from Ceres's workshop, loaded with the Queen's Tail and with Water Serpent Scales affixed to it. Our other party members headed out to the labyrinth entrance in advance, while Madoka—who'd be using the cart—Cion, and I stayed back to hear the rundown from McCain.

"I installed the Magical Bonnet Canopy your merchant here requested yesterday; it added an extra day's worth of work to the whole enterprise, but it's good to go. You're gonna be the one driving, right, little lady? It's got an Acceleration Stone built in, so it should run under its own power—just be careful not to use up all its magic."

"Thank you; I will!"

"You shouldn't have any problem if someone riding in the cart can keep it charged up with magic, so be resourceful. If you happen to know anyone who can lend you some horsepower, you could pull the thing that way, too."

"Woof."

Cion could certainly pull the cart if it came to that, but I figured it would be best to rely on the Acceleration Stone and let the cart propel itself. That way Cion could guard it and stay ready for action, just in case.

"If you can summon me, I'd be glad to pull the cart."

"Ah, we might take you up on that," I said, answering Alphecca's voice.

Having Alphecca tow the cart would be our fastest option for sure. Then again, I didn't know how likely it was that the cargo could withstand the acceleration from a Banish Burst, so I didn't want to push it.

"Thanks a lot, McCain."

"Don't mention it. Come and see me if you need anything else—maintenance, improvements, anything like that. If you've got the materials, I'll whip you up any kinda cart you want."

McCain stuck out his hand for a handshake. When I offered mine, he smiled broadly enough to show his white teeth, then left the rented workshop.

"First of all, let's give the Queen's Tail a test run."

"It's such a big, um... What is it, again? It's an amazing weapon, either way..."

It looked like the Nine-Tail that we'd taken from The Calamity made up the weapon's barrel. Its pipework connected to the power source: the Queen Scorpion's Afterglow. I could really sense Ceres and Steiner's excellent craftsmanship. You could call it a work of art.

"It certainly looks very, very powerful...but I'd like to check and make sure just how powerful it is. We need to be aware of what it's capable of."

"Understood... Besides, I'd like to get used to it so that I'm not caught by surprise when we shoot it for real."

"Woof!"

"All right, then—mind giving us a lift to the front of the labyrinth?"

Once Ceres and Steiner were aboard the cart, too, we used the Acceleration Stone. It was fitted with a dial that let us set its speed, from about typical walking speed to a full-on sprint. There was also a steering wheel to set the cart's direction, though it looked like it would take a lot of strength to turn.

"I think I can manage to drive it, Arihito. What do you say…? Are we ready to go?"

"Take it away, Madoka. Keep it reasonably slow to start with so we can see how much magic it consumes."

Technically speaking, the road was paved, but there were a lot of spots where it wasn't level. We started driving slowly down the bumpy road. Looking at Madoka's license, I could see that, at around walking speed, the cart didn't use up enough magic for us to worry about.

"That McCain's quite a craftsman. I guess it's no surprise that someone with a shop in District Five is more skilled than we are."

"But he did praise our work on the Queen's Tail, Master! He seems like a nice guy."

I agreed with Steiner, but I was too busy concentrating on Madoka's driving to chime in. However, it turned out she was a very safe driver, so I didn't have any advice to give. Actually, come to think of it, Madoka was probably better at driving than I was.

"I know it's powered by magic, but it feels an awful lot like a car, doesn't it? It might even be a smoother ride."

"You're right… I never thought I'd ride a vehicle like this in the Labyrinth Country."

Cion took the lead; we drove behind her all the way to the plaza in front of the entrance to the Blazing Red Mansion. There we found not only the rest of our party and Ferris, but also Khosrow and Kozelka, as well as Ivril and Viola (whom we'd contacted the night before) and Third Class Dragon Captain Nayuta.

"You arrived earlier than I expected, Mr. Arihito, but you'll find that we are always ready to assist you. Please direct me as you will today."

"Thanks, Ivril, but I hope you'll hold tight just a little longer. There's something I want to do before we face the Simian Lord."

"We'll have to fully appraise the current situation before we put together a plan. The Simian Lord is a cunning monster... We've already fought it once; we can expect it to be ready for round two."

The Simian Lord's stronghold had been set with traps to draw in and catch Seekers. It seemed very likely that those traps had been laid again in order to protect the Simian Lord and enlarge the ranks of subordinated Seekers.

As you'd guess from its colossal size, the Simian Lord had superhuman strength—enough to restrain Alphecca with chains and drag her in. The chains it tossed out with its Concealed Weapon Cast skill were made of Helltect Steel; Murakumo could cut through it, if Ariadne's Guard Arm did the swinging, but there was a chance even Murakumo might get shattered if it tried to cut its way out again.

On top of that, the Simian Lord could use its Demon Hand skill to deflect long-range attacks. My own magical bullets hadn't gotten through. We would clearly need to come up with some way to make projectile attacks hit. I thought that my usual strategy of applying my Attack Support skill to boost striking attacks might be effective.

As its full name, Shining Simian Lord, would suggest, it could wield fire, too. The defensive equipment we'd acquired thus far would keep us covered against fire elemental damage to some extent, but we were still better off trying to avoid its stronger moves entirely. If we couldn't help but get hit, we'd have to rely on several overlapping defensive skills.

"First things first, we'll have to pinpoint the Simian Lord itself. It doesn't mean a thing to just take down a double. We'll ascertain where the real Simian Lord is, and the very moment we find it, those of us with the most firepower will act. In our party, that's Elitia."

"Indeed... We can handle Named Monster underlings, but going by what I've seen of Elitia, I believe she's better suited to play the part of main attacker. I'd say our specialties lie more in keeping foes entangled."

That would certainly be useful when it came time to nullify the Seekers under the Simian Lord's command. I'd count on Ivril and Viola for that.

"I beg your pardon, Mr. Atobe. Under Third Class Dragon Major Dylan's orders, I'll be participating in this mission as well."

"I appreciate it. But what about Commander Dylan...?"

"He sends his regrets that he is not able to participate in person. Unfortunately, that is all I know about the matter."

I suspected the Guild Saviors had their own opinions on how

the Simian Lord had been left unhandled; with that in mind, it wasn't surprising that they'd sent Nayuta to join us. I supposed it didn't hurt that they'd also get a full report of the battle this way, either.

I was happy to have as many people fighting on our side as we could get. I'd seen how strong Nayuta really was, and I knew she'd make a reliable ally in combat.

"We'll need to start by gathering information so we can form a strategy. I'd like you to enter the labyrinth with me, Nayuta."

"Roger that."

"If you're gathering intel, I'm your girl, Mr. Atobe. Will you put me to work?" Adeline asked as she stepped out from behind Seraphina. Her skills were indeed very useful for scouting the surrounding geography.

"...That suit looks good on you, Arihito," said Elitia.

At first I thought, *Why now, of all times?* But then I realized that might have been exactly the reason—Elitia was trying to calm some of the nerves running through the party.

"I never thought I'd wind up wearing a suit this fancy, to be honest."

"Why not? It's perfect for you!" said Igarashi.

"Yeah! I mean, the way you wear a suit is, like, a huge part of what makes you seem so reliable, Ari-poo!"

"That's right," Suzuna agreed. "The jet-black color really gives you a composed air."

"Thanks, guys... Anyway, look. It's time we went to rescue Rury. We're gonna free Theresia from her hex, too. So, shall we?"

""""Yessir!""""

The first time we encountered the Simian Lord, all we could do was run away. This time would be different.

Theresia walked slightly ahead of me with her Curse Eater weapon—the Gloria Stiletto—in hand. Soon, I thought, she'd be using it to cut down the Simian Lord that had hexed her; that was a sight I wanted her to see.

CHAPTER 4

Simian Showdown in the Blazing Red Mansion

Part I: Siege Weaponry

We entered the Blazing Red Mansion at the first floor and moved through its forest of autumnal leaves. When I looked up, it was as if the world were soaked in orange. It struck me that back in Japan, I might have seen the same view looking out over trees at sunset in autumn. The only difference was that these trees were on an entirely different scale.

There was no sign of any monsters, but according to Nayuta, that didn't mean that none would show up. Side paths led off to areas where we'd likely find them.

"Don't these look like shrine gates back in Japan? I noticed them last time we were here."

"They do… I wonder if it's a coincidence. I doubt they were made for the same reason as shrine gates."

Suzuna and Igarashi were talking about a line of metal pillars that were all painted red. Passing through them teleported us to the second floor. A few steps beyond, the scene opened up; where nothing had been visible previously, there ran a great river with strongholds to the east and west. This was all familiar, except for one major difference: This time, there was a stronghold in the center, too.

"A new fortress... How'd it get built in so little time?"

"That must be the stronghold the Simian Lord originally wanted... Not that I know that for sure. Either way, it looks like it was built to be especially difficult to attack."

We'd have to cross the river and make our way through the area beyond it before we had any hope of assailing the stronghold walls.

"I'll check the land around us one more time. There may be more changes than we can see from the surface."

"Thanks, Adeline. Please do."

Adeline spun the handle on her bowgun and aimed it up toward the sky.

"Arrow filled with my magic, take this momentary life and become my obedient familiar!"

◆Current Status◆
> ADELINE activated ARROW FAMILIAR ⟶ Created 1 FAMILIAR ARROW
> ADELINE activated SEARCH ARROW ⟶ Fired FAMILIAR ARROW

"You can see the lay of the land through your license. It looks like part of the view is obstructed, though."

The strongholds to the east and west were simple wooden structures. The gate that led to them was made of wood, too, and it opened with a mechanism. It wasn't shut, though. The central stronghold didn't appear to have a front entrance of its own, but if we took the long way around, there was another gate into it in the back. However, that gate was right on a cliff, so it didn't seem like a smart way in for us. The risk of anti-aerial defenses was too great for us to attempt flying in, either—not to mention that the whole party wouldn't be able to fly in in the first place.

"The gate's not closed… It's trying to lure us in. Either that, or we're too strong for the gate to be worth closing in the first place…"

"Forget that for a moment… Look there, by the gates at the backs of the east and west strongholds."

"There's one Simian Lord in each… Maybe one of them is the real one and the other's a double…?"

"……"

"…Theresia?"

"Theresia might be able to recognize the monster that hexed her," said Ceres.

If she was right, then Theresia could tell us what to make of these two Simian Lords.

Theresia shook her head slowly.

"If we trust Theresia's senses, then neither one is the real Simian Lord, Arihito. I take it one is the monster they call the Demon Monkey Guard. Which would mean the other one's probably another underling of the Simian Lord that hasn't been identified yet."

I wondered if Elitia had seen this double when she'd been in the labyrinth before.

"It's unlikely that two monsters with the same name exist at the same time. If you beat a Named Monster, then another one pops up with the same name after a while, right? In that case…"

"The Simian Lord has two Named Monster underlings. It's possible either or both is a double. And now they're guarding the way into the central stronghold."

If what Seraphina said was correct, then we had to consider what the Simian Lord would do while we were fighting one of these guards. Assuming its main goal was survival, there was a good chance that it would flee while we fought the double.

"May I see that, too, Mr. Arihito?"

"…S-sure, sorry. This is information everyone should know, after all."

"Would you share that map data, Adeline?"

"Roger. Apologies; that would have been sensible."

Adeline shared the map data with everyone involved in our strategy. Ivril and Viola took out their Seeker's licenses; they were different colors from ours and looked like they were made out of different materials.

"If there are two doubles, that's evidence that neither one of these is the real Simian Lord. Still, anything can happen in a labyrinth… Even knowing the lay of the land in advance, it would be difficult for a Seeker seeing them for the first time to tell real from fake. Arihito and his party have encountered the Simian

Lord before; that makes it all the more important not to fall for the enemy's plan."

"Elitia is the one who saw the double. Without her bringing us that information, we might have found ourselves in a tight spot..."

"That doesn't change the fact that I was reckless...but I'm glad the intel on the Double skill was useful. Now let me fill you in on the other Seekers the Simian Lord has under its control."

There were three Seekers with simian masks, plus Rury, who stayed beside the Simian Lord to keep it healed up—but they weren't the only ones. Elitia also spotted a party of four male Seekers. Garf and Kazan had been charmed by the enemy, and the other two were otherwise incapacitated. It seemed entirely likely that the four of them were under the Simian Lord's command.

"So there's the Dancer, the Martial Artist, the Terraformer, and the Healer...plus four more men. Were they the only ones you confirmed?"

"Yes, that's all I saw," said Elitia. "Is there something you know, Ivril?"

"Someone I knew, rather. I'm looking for a member that our party lost when we faced the Simian Lord some time ago. A Puppeteer woman."

Not only Ivril but also Viola looked toward me, as if they were trying to show their true intentions. The two of them had lost someone important to them—and they wanted to get her back. In other words, they were in the same situation as Elitia.

"Although we've confirmed that she's still alive, we haven't been able to clear the Simian Lord's stronghold. The Simian Lord didn't even show himself in front of me... Far from it, in fact; what we thought was our enemy's base was just a fake, there to camouflage the real one."

Ivril pointed right across the river. Her finger indicated a building separate from the Simian Lord's fortress.

"Is that so...?"

"Perhaps that fortress wall was built as some sort of test. It bears a striking likeness to the central stronghold's walls—at least on the outside."

"So you're saying that it built a small stronghold at first, then changed to building a larger one?"

With that kind of behavior, it seemed the Simian Lord meant to make a castle of the entire region. True to its reputation as an evil overlord, the Simian Lord was trying to rebuild the whole labyrinth floor as its own territory.

"If what you say is true, Ivril, then it seems the real Simian Lord will escape while we fight its doubles."

"Or perhaps it intends to ambush us with a challenge... It's of utmost importance that we eliminate the *real* Simian Lord. To do that, we'll have to take it by surprise and somehow disperse its army of underlings."

"Disperse, huh...? Right now, there are seventeen of us, not including support staff. If possible, Adeline, I think you should hang back and hold tight with the support crew, since you can keep abreast of the situation over a wide area."

"Roger that. I'll be ready to use my Familiar Arrow to scope out the situation and keep everybody informed."

"So you're in the waitin' squad with the rest of us, huh?" said Ceres. "Good to have you aboard, Adeline."

"Y-yes, ma'am! I must say, meeting a jade here is an unexpected honor!"

"I'm really not that big a deal… Don't let fantasies go to your head, you hear?"

Ceres fixed her pointed hat atop her head and got back on the cart with Madoka at the wheel.

"Arihito, I found us the perfect target for testing out the Queen's Tail."

"…Would that be the smaller fortress, Ceres?"

"That's the one. The Simian Lord's stronghold hasn't shown any sign of acknowledging us, even though we've made it to the front lawn, so to speak, and are getting ready to storm the place… A little funny, don't you think?"

Ceres's grin hardly seemed to suit the situation. Khosrow and Kozelka seemed to think it was interesting, too, but all they did was look in our direction and nod before turning back to stare balefully at the central fortress.

"We'll stand on lookout here, Mr. Atobe."

"Thank you. All right, everyone—wait here for a moment."

With that parting message to our allies, Madoka, Ceres, and I headed off to where the small stronghold was marked on the map.

The sound of the river grew fainter and fainter until it disappeared. A wide, barren region stretched out in the middle of the forest, and there stood a wall formed primarily of rough, unworked stone.

The Simian Lord had burned down part of the woods and attempted to build a fortress there. Perhaps something like it had been there from the very start; either way, just as Ivril had said, the stone wall bore a striking resemblance to the architecture of the central fortress.

"All right, then," said Ceres. "This time around, we'll try attacking with my magic, Arihito. Madoka, are you all set?"

"Yes, whenever you're ready..."

"Here goes... I'm gonna start charging the Queen's Tail with magic!"

Ceres's magic linked up with the Queen Scorpion's Afterglow and began flowing through the two metal pipes. The weapon consumed a great deal of magic, but Ceres on her own could provide enough to fire it.

"This should put its output at around eighty percent... Fire it off at full power, and it'll take too long to cool down again. Okay, here we go!"

"Roger!"

"Give it a shot, Ceres!"

"Fire!"

The Queen Scorpion's Afterglow pulsated. Then a bright light like a brilliant comet shot out of the barrel formed from the Nine-Tail. It zoomed upward, then, after a moment of building up power, flew toward the stone wall, tracing an arc through the air as if it were a living thing.

◆Current Status◆
> CERES used ★QUEEN'S TAIL +1 to activate
  STING RAY ⟶ Terrain: Rampart successfully
  destroyed

Nine bolts of light, arranged in a thick bundle, pierced through the stone wall of the small stronghold. Rough as it was, the wall appeared hard to destroy; however, not only did the Queen's Tail blow through a section of it, but the damage also spread to a wide area around the point of impact. Only an oval-shaped crater was left. Madoka and I were at a loss for words—actually, so was Ceres, who had fired the Queen's Tail herself. The three of us were shocked by its destructive power.

◆Current Status◆
> ★QUEEN'S TAIL +1 commenced cooldown
Capable of refiring in 500 seconds

Smoke wafted up from the white-hot barrel. It looked like you'd be lucky to get off with a serious burn if you'd touched it. Its cooldown time was relatively short, all things considered; Ceres and Steiner had thought to include a magic stone–driven cooling system.

"Um... Well... That was pretty amazing...," I managed. "So amazing, it might be enough to beat that monster on its own..."

"It's particularly effective against buildings. It still packs a punch against monsters, too, but it'll fall to pieces against any foe with half-decent evasive skills," Ceres explained. "It's going to need some extra finagling to improve its precision if we're gonna use it as our ace in the hole."

"That makes sense," said Madoka. "But still, if it can destroy walls like that, it could catch the Simian Lord off guard, at least."

Without a word, Ceres gave Madoka a pat on the shoulder. I guess Madoka figured out what the gesture meant, because she immediately began driving the cart back to the rest of our party.

Up until that point, it hadn't occurred to me that we could attack the stronghold itself. But now, spurred by the information we'd received, an idea was forming in my mind. I'd have to run it by my allies, hear their thoughts, and decide whether it was really worth a shot, though. It all came down to how they received it.

To start with, I divided the group into four smaller parties. I put these parties together based on who could most easily exert their full power at the time, but I still kept an eye on overall balance, too.

```
◆Party 1◆
1: Kozelka      Master Fencer      Level 13
2: Nayuta       Scout              Level 12
3: Kyouka       Valkyrie           Level 8
```

4: Cion	Silver Hound	Level 8
5: Misaki	Gambler	Level 7
6: Suzuna	Shrine Maiden	Level 7

◆Party 2◆

1: Khosrow	Gladiator	Level 13
2: Feresia	Felid Fighter	Level 12
3: Melissa	Dissector	Level 8
4: Ivril	Job Concealed	Level 12
5: Viola	Job Concealed	Level 12

◆Party 3◆

1: Arihito	※αΩ^	Level 8
2: Elitia	Flawless Knight	Level 11
3: Seraphina	Riot Soldier	Level 12
4: Theresia	Rogue	Level 8
5: Madoka	Merchant	Level 5

◆Party 4◆

1: Ceres	Runemaker	Level 5
2: Chiara	Blacksmith	Level 4
3: Luca	Tailor	Level 7
4: Adeline	Hunter	Level 8

There were several jobs among our crew that I had never seen before, but what really stood out was the lack of information about Ivril and Viola. I wondered if they kept their jobs hidden of their own volition. That was at least what "Job Concealed" seemed to imply if I took it at face value.

Steiner was registered under their real name, Chiara. When we'd fought together before, I hadn't had the time to check and see. Steiner looked embarrassed to have that name out there, but they at least seemed to understand that it was inevitable.

"I know we'll be waiting back here, Arihito," said Luca, "but I can't help but notice that if a monster does show up, we're not going to be able to do much other than buy time... Is that going to be all right?"

"Sure. Don't push yourselves too hard. As long as you can neutralize the subjugated Seekers, that is... It's not going to be easy, but I'm going to need you to watch out for them."

"Really, we'd ideally mobilize a whole squad of Guild Saviors to deal with this," said Adeline. "I'm sorry we couldn't bring an entire unit along."

"Not at all—I'm grateful enough just to have all of you here. More grateful than I can say."

"You've nothing to thank us for," said Kozelka. "We are all here by choice."

"There's a rule that we're not supposed to take sides with any particular party, y'know," Khosrow added. "It was the Guild that wanted you guys to come to District Five in the first place, though. They'll let this slide if we pass it off as helping out a party that's contributing to the Guild."

Nayuta nodded as Kozelka and Khosrow spoke. Adeline gave a respectful bow. As she watched the four of them, Seraphina laughed quietly.

"Thank you all so much. If I may be so bold as to say so in Mr. Atobe's place, that is."

"You're more than welcome to, Seraphina," I told her. "We wouldn't have made it this far if it weren't for you."

"Mr. Atobe…"

"Lieutenant Seraphina excels at defensive maneuvers. I'm a 'bulwark on the front lines' kinda guy myself, but in terms of sheer impenetrable defense, she's got me beat."

"…You flatter me, Dragon Sergeant Khosrow."

"Anyway, Atobe. You've got us split up into groups. How do you want us to play this?"

"Right! First of all, I want Kozelka's team and Khosrow's team to engage the Simian Lord doubles at the east and west strongholds."

The plan was for them to break into both strongholds at the same time, drawing the attention of both doubles. While they were doing that, my team could use the Queen's Tail and start exercising our real firepower. We'd eventually reach the Simian Lord, which I expected would be staying at a safe distance while its subordinates protected the strongholds.

"Mr. Atobe, I'm sure you have your reasons for splitting us up this way, but if I may ask a question: Why is the team you've put together to fight the Simian Lord the one with the lowest average level…?"

"When Elitia and I put the teams together, we figured that we were likely to have stronger instantaneous strikes than any other pairing. With Seraphina helping us out with defense, we'll be able to stand toe-to-toe with the higher ranks. Add Madoka with the Queen's Tail, and Theresia, who's absolutely essential to the plan's success, and we've got the smallest number of people we need. The cart's a limiting factor; if too many people are in it, Madoka won't be able to steer as dexterously."

"I see. That makes sense. Like I said, Lieutenant Seraphina has me beat for defense, and I'll grant Elitia's got the superior attack power, too... With you as a conductor to bring out their strengths, Atobe, I guess you won't be missing anything the other teams have got."

"I want to do as much as we can to keep the Seekers that the Simian Lord has subjugated safe and alive, too. That means the stronger the teams infiltrating the east and west strongholds are, the better. Fighting to nullify an enemy is harder than regular combat."

I knew I was forcing Kozelka's and Khosrow's teams into a tough scuffle. That's why I'd made sure to fill their ranks with people with skills that would help nullify enemies, in addition to strong fighters.

"Once those teams have engaged with the enemy at the east and west strongholds, we can expect the central stronghold to be on the alert for invaders of its own. We'll act as a sort of third arrow to strike from outside their guard."

"Let's call it Operation Third Arrow, then. Roger that, Mr. Atobe. My team and I will assault the eastern stronghold."

"And we'll take the west. I'll be in touch once we're in position, Adeline."

"Y-yes, sir! You can count on me to help both of your teams synchronize your attacks!" Adeline saluted Kozelka and Khosrow. Then all of them turned to face me.

"All right, everyone... The plan is underway. Once you're all done, we'll regroup at this same spot."

""""Roger!""""

My party members answered in unison. The other participants responded, too—and with that, Kozelka and Khosrow's teams were on the move.

"Okay, then," I said. "Let's get going, too."

"At what point will we be storming the stronghold?" Elitia asked me.

"Once the doubles are dealt with. Adeline will keep us filled in on Kozelka and Khosrow's maneuvers—"

"*Arihito, since there is at least one member of your party in each team, I will be able to keep you informed of the conditions of battle as well.*"

"Ariadne..."

Hearing Ariadne's choice of words—"conditions of battle"—I had a sudden thought. There would surely be a moment at which all of our allies who were storming the east and west strongholds would have their backs facing me. Which meant I could use my support skills on them. As they fought to expose the Simian Lord's doubles and free the subordinated Seekers, I would do as much as I possibly could to help.

"Looks like you've got something on your mind again, Arihito..."

"Just thinking about how there's something I can do specifically *because* I'm here on the back lines. That's my job as a Rearguard to a T."

"…Every time you smile like that, you go on to pull off something seriously amazing."

Elitia was smiling, too. She was exactly right; what we needed for the battle ahead of us wasn't anger or regret.

It was the knowledge of what we would win when the fighting was over that would give us the continued will to press on to victory.

Part II: Playing Parts

Ariadne kept me abreast of Kozelka and Khosrow's movements. She kept me up to date with real-time information and geographical data from Adeline.

"*I shall help you consider this information so that it can be processed in tandem.*"

"Ah… Thanks. If they can't keep the Simian Lord's doubles completely distracted, then we might have a more chaotic battle than we bargained for on our hands when they fall back."

"*I will pinpoint the moment at which the Simian Lord can neither fall back nor enter formation with its underlings.*"

Suzuna was on Kozelka's team, and Melissa was on Khosrow's; it was as if I could see what the two of them saw, out of either corner of my vision. I tried to follow each team's movements intently, even as I was amazed that the Hidden Gods' power allowed me to do so.

"I'm going to cut my way into their ranks! The rest of you, follow behind me!"

"Y-yes, ma'am!"

Kozelka ran much faster than Igarashi or Misaki could—faster even than Suzuna on Cion's back. Nayuta, however, managed to keep up with Kozelka.

Beyond a bridge across the river stood the gate to the strongholds. Someone had made their way into a nearby turret; Kozelka seemed to notice this, but she didn't slow her pace as she ran through the gate.

"Kozelka, look!" Suzuna cried.

The instant all of them were through the gate, which was made from logs lashed together, it closed.

Beyond the gate, there was a wide plaza where the ground rose up into several square pillars. Those pillars hadn't been present in the aerial view I'd seen earlier.

We saw that the Simian Lord does have a Terraformer under its control... Maybe they can make obstacles like these.

"Is this some kind of trap...? The Simian Lord's trying to capture more Seekers, then. Awfully greedy, isn't it?"

Kozelka drew her sword. As a small, preemptive action, Nayuta tossed something upward: a rope with a weight attached to the end. In a flash, the rope wrapped around the person in the turret above.

```
◆Current Status◆
> Nayuta activated Rope Bind ⟶ Simian Lord Minion:
  Hunter was restrained
```

The skill Nayuta used was like Adeline's—shared by Scouts and Hunters.

"Wow...," Igarashi marveled. "Nayuta's really, *really* handy with that rope..."

"Please take care! There are enemies in those pillars' shadows!"

```
◆Monsters Encountered◆
★Shining Simian Lord
Level 12
Hostile
Fire Resistant
Dropped Loot: ???
Simian Lord Minion: Hunter
Level 11
Restrained
Dropped Loot: ???
Simian Lord Minion: Assassin
Level 11
Hostile
Dropped Loot: ???
Evil Ape A
Level 10
```

```
Hostile
Dropped Loot: ???
EVIL APE B
Level 10
Hostile
Dropped Loot: ???
```

This Simian Lord wasn't the real thing. At least that's what our reading told us, though it was hard to know for sure while it was obscured behind the pillars. The enemies Kozelka's team encountered also didn't include the Terraformer, who must have moved elsewhere. Instead, another shadow was visible in the area shown by Adeline's Familiar Arrow.

"KIKIII...!"

"Careful, Ms. Kyouka! One got past me!"

```
◆Current Status◆
> KOZELKA activated FLASH FEND ⟶ Hit EVIL APE A
EVIL APE A was knocked back
```

"GIII...!"

Kozelka crossed one of the Evil Apes, slashing it hard enough to send it flying as she went. However, the other one leaped out from the shadow of a pillar and headed right for Igarashi.

```
◆Current Status◆
> EVIL APE B attacked
> KYOUKA activated MIRAGE STEP ⟶ Evaded attack
```

"It's not over yet, Kyouka...!" Suzuna cried.

"Kngh!"

"Awoooooo!"

Igarashi dodged the Evil Ape's first attack, but it stayed on her and immediately struck again. That was Mirage Step's weakness: It wasn't useful for avoiding multiple successive attacks. Luckily, Cion wasn't about to let Igarashi get hurt.

◆Current Status◆
> Cion activated Shoulder Tackle
> Evil Ape B activated Backward Roll ⟶ Evaded attack

The Evil Ape somersaulted backward very quickly—quickly enough to avoid Cion's tackle. It hung back beside one of the square land pillars with its claws out, grinning at Suzuna on Cion's back as it waited.

Misaki, throw your cards!

"...Hyeaaaugh!"

Misaki was positioned in front of me. That meant I could check her status—and make good use of my skills.

◆Current Status◆
> Arihito activated Outside Assist
> Evil Ape B activated Triangular Leap
> Arihito activated Attack Support 2 ⟶ Support Type: Force Shot: Stun
> Misaki activated Thunder Joker ⟶ Hit Evil Ape B

Evil Ape B was Stunned
Canceled Triangular Leap

"What just happened, Misaki?"

"I heard Arihito's voice… It was, like, just like always, with him watching over me from behind!"

"Hyaaaaaah!"

◆Current Status◆
> Kozelka activated Triple Wolf Fang Thrust → Hit
  Evil Ape B
Evil Ape B was knocked back
> Simian Lord Minion: Assassin stopped hiding
> Simian Lord Minion: Assassin activated Backstab →
  Targeted Kozelka for double damage

Kozelka, behind you!

"…!"

◆Current Status◆
> Kozelka activated Direwolf's Instinct →
  Immediate action enabled
> Kozelka activated Dark Haze → Evaded Backstab
> Simian Lord Minion: Assassin activated Obsessive
  Pursuit
> Kozelka activated Parry → Nullified Obsessive
  Pursuit
Simian Lord Minion: Assassin was rendered
  defenseless

The enemy attempted to immediately follow the first attack with another, yet Kozelka reacted as if she'd perfectly anticipated the move. The Assassin had attempted to backstab her, but instead, Kozelka left them wide open.

"There!"

◆Current Status◆
> KOZELKA activated WEAPON HUNT ⟶ SIMIAN LORD
  MINION: ASSASSIN was disarmed
> NAYUTA activated ROPE BIND ⟶ SIMIAN LORD MINION:
  ASSASSIN was restrained

"That's two down... I restrained the Assassin, Kozelka!"

"Please stay on guard, everyone! I can't see the double anywhere!"

"GWOOOAAAH!"

A mighty roar echoed through the clearing where the countless pillars stood, strong enough to shake the ground. A gut feeling drove me to shout out as well.

Igarashi, use Decoy and Force Target! And please get some distance after you've got them set up!

"Everyone, get out of here!"

◆Current Status◆
> KYOUKA activated DECOY and FORCE TARGET
> ★SHINING SIMIAN LORD activated BOUNDING BOULDER
  BREAKER ⟶ DECOY was destroyed
Terrain features within range were destroyed
> Terrain collapse caused rockslides

The enormous ape leaped down from atop one of the pillars, slamming its fist into the ground as it landed. A shock wave passed through the area, cracking the stone pillars and sending them tumbling down in an instant.

"Ms. Kyouka!"

"Aiieee! S-Suzu!"

"Woof!"

◆Current Status◆
> Cion activated Disaster Preparedness ⟶ Speed increased
Reduced slowing effects of obstacles
> Cion activated Emergency Extraction ⟶ Targets: Kyouka, Misaki, Suzuna

Cion ran into the fray to rescue Igarashi, Misaki, and Suzuna. Nayuta had one end of her rope tied around a stake and she flung it toward a stone pillar, while Kozelka used her own physical prowess to escape the destruction.

"Grrrrrr..."

"GIII!"

The monster that my license identified as the Simian Lord gave some sort of order to the Evil Apes. They grabbed the tied-up Assassin and started to leave with him in tow.

"You're not getting away!"

"GISHAAAH!"

Evil Ape B, the more wounded of the pair, took the Assassin, while the remaining one leaped toward Kozelka to strike. She warded it off with her sword and jumped back, putting distance between her and the ape.

At that moment, what had been a colossal, red-furred ape began changing form.

"GWOOOAAAHHH!"

◆Current Status◆
> ★Shining Simian Lord deactivated Double ⟶
  Transformed into ★Stonesplitting Savage Simian
> ★Stonesplitting Savage Simian activated Bloody
  Battle Roar
> Evil Ape A's attack power and speed
  drastically increased
Defense power decreased

As if to acknowledge that Kozelka's team were foes that must be destroyed, the giant ape revealed its true form—ash-gray fur, scars over its eye and all. It roared yet again. At the sound of its battle cry, the Evil Apes' eyes turned red and the fur all over their bodies bristled. They looked even more ferocious than before.

"…You must let us through. Try to impede us, and we shall show no mercy."

The Savage Simian merely grinned at Kozelka's threat. It seemed to relish the thought of battle.

As Kozelka's team entered the eastern stronghold, Khosrow and his crew crossed their bridge and broke into the western one. They found a wide courtyard surrounded by a wall formed of logs driven straight into the ground and a brazier lit with flame. It looked very much like a gladiatorial arena—an image supported by the enormous, red-furred ape seated at the end of the yard with its chin in its hands.

"This stronghold you've got here is awful big to have so few people in it... Where'd all your captured Seekers go? I thought there was supposed to be ten of 'em!"

```
◆Monsters Encountered◆
★Shining Simian Lord
Level 12
Hostile
Fire Resistant
Dropped Loot: ???
Simian Lord Minion: Dancer
Level 11
Hostile
Dropped Loot: ???
Simian Lord Minion: Martial Artist
Level 11
Hostile
Dropped Loot: ???
Warrior Ape
Level 11
Hostile
Dropped Loot: ???
Sorcerer Ape
```

Level 11
Hostile
Dropped Loot: ???

Khosrow spit those words, demonstrating his fighting spirit for all to see. The Warrior Ape strode out to challenge him, as if compelled by the force of his taunt.

◆Current Status◆
> WARRIOR APE activated GRAPPLE ⟶ Opposing
  KHOSROW with brute force

The Warrior Ape had an unusually muscular upper body. Its raw strength made it a fitting rival for even the level-13 Khosrow.

"So that skill forces me into close combat with you, huh?" Khosrow asked the ape.

"GIII!!"

◆Current Status◆
> SORCERER APE activated BALEFUL WORD
> SIMIAN LORD MINION: DANCER activated ENTRANCING
  DANCE

The Sorcerer Ape—clad in rags and leaning on a crooked wooden staff—chanted something. Black letters formed from magical energy appeared at the tip of its staff, then sailed through the air toward Khosrow. As if that weren't enough, the subordinated Dancer began dancing—but then...

◆Current Status◆
> VETERAN'S TALISMAN effects activated ⟶ KHOSROW
  resisted Charm

"You're gonna need way, way more than that to tempt me!"

◆Current Status◆
> KHOSROW deactivated GRAPPLE
> KHOSROW activated BATTLE CRY ⟶ Party
  members' attack and defense power
  increased
> IVRIL activated REFLECTIVE PARASOL ⟶ Reflected
  BALEFUL WORD
> BALEFUL WORD hit SIMIAN LORD MINION: DANCER
SIMIAN LORD MINION: DANCER's attack, defense, and
  speed decreased

Khosrow jumped back, breaking free from the Warrior Ape's clutches. Ivril, who'd been holding her ground in the center ranks, stepped forward to deflect Baleful Word with her parasol. The ability bounced harmlessly away from its target and struck the subordinated Dancer instead.

"You can reflect attacks back at the bad guys, huh? Not bad, lady!"

"Let that show you that neither gender nor age means a thing on the battlefield."

Ivril, look out on your right!

"...!!"

◆Current Status◆
> Simian Lord Minion: Martial Artist activated Verge
  of Nothingness ⟶ Reduced presence
Raised success rate of surprise attacks
> Simian Lord Minion: Martial Artist activated Swift
  Arrow Step
> Feresia activated Interception ⟶ Target: Simian
  Lord Minion: Martial Artist
> Feresia activated Insulating Palm ⟶ Nullified
  Swift Arrow Step

The Martial Artist's presence seemed to fade away into nothingness, even though he remained right there. He stepped toward
Ivril to strike so swiftly that it didn't seem physically possible—
but Ferris darted between them and blocked his blows with her
palms just in the nick of time.

"Mrrrowr!!"

"—?!"

◆Current Status◆
> Feresia activated Impact Pad ⟶ Hit Simian Lord
  Minion: Martial Artist
Simian Lord Minion: Martial Artist was knocked back
  and Concussed

*Now that's strong... She nullified his attack with the pad of her
paw, then struck right back at him through his defenses without
mercy. Amazing what a level-12 Felid Fighter can do!*

"Viola!"

◆Current Status◆
> Viola activated Serpent Bind ⟶ Simian Lord
  Minion: Martial Artist was restrained
> Viola activated Paralyzing Venom ⟶ Simian Lord
  Minion: Martial Artist was paralyzed
> Simian Lord Minion: Dancer activated Throwing
  Dagger ⟶ Durability of Viola's ★Great Violet
  Serpent's Poison Whip was reduced

Viola's weapon was a whip that she kept at the ready in her skirt. She drew it out and immediately used it to restrain the Martial Artist, hitting him with paralyzing poison in the process. The Dancer attempted to cut the whip apart and free the Martial Artist, but one attack wasn't enough to do the job.

"KIIIKIIIII!!"

◆Current Status◆
> Warrior Ape activated Cruel Bite
> Khosrow activated Max Counter ⟶ Hit Warrior Ape
Significant knockback

The Warrior Ape aimed for Viola in an attempt to free the Martial Artist from his restraints. However, Khosrow anticipated its movement and countered with an explosively powerful attack. The Warrior Ape was about the size of a full-grown adult human, but Khosrow's counter still sent it flying away.

"GIIIII!"

"Too bad for you...I'm still here."

◆Current Status◆
> Sorcerer Ape activated Scream of Animosity
> Melissa attacked ⟶ Activated effects of
  Ambush
Critical hit on Sorcerer Ape
Sorcerer Ape's action was canceled
> Feresia activated Leg Cannon ⟶ Hit Sorcerer Ape
Significant knockback

First Melissa prevented the Sorcerer Ape's action, then Ferris immediately followed up with an attack. They were completely in sync, like only a mother and daughter could be. Khosrow's team clearly had complete control over the situation; they didn't need any of my support. They had already put the Martial Artist and the monsters out of commission, and thanks to the reflected Baleful Word, the remaining Dancer's movements were slow and dull.

However, Khosrow's expression was still strained.

"Why won't these guys stay down? How can they keep getting back up?"

The Simian Lord seated at the far end of the arena was, as we'd imagined, the second double. Its red fur turned to black as its body shrank.

◆Current Status◆
> ★Shining Simian Lord deactivated Double ⟶
  Transformed into ★Demon Monkey Guard
> ★Demon Monkey Guard activated Peon's Fate

> Warrior Ape and Sorcerer Ape transformed into
  War Puppets

Khosrow's team ran into just about the same situation as Kozelka's team; the Stonesplitting Savage Simian and Demon Monkey Guard both powered up their monster underlings and looked determined to fight to the end. Not only that, but the two of them were starting to move themselves. With the Double skill deactivated, they could no longer mimic the Simian Lord's abilities, but on the other hand, they could now use their own inherent powers.

"Looks like we've got the real fight on our hands now," said Khosrow. "We can't let these guys make it back to the Simian Lord, Atobe. Make sure you take it down before we regroup!"

Right! Stay safe, Khosrow!

"You got it!" Khosrow raised his fist to meet mine.

Then he made a mad dash to the front line, slashing away the reinvigorated Warrior Ape as he went, to face the Demon Monkey Guard.

Part III: Bloodbath

The two doubles had revealed their true forms, and Kozelka's and Khosrow's teams kept on fighting to stop them from regrouping with the Simian Lord.

"The contract holders have spent the required time in battle. Alphecca may now be summoned."

That was how we'd get our cart across the river—by calling on Alphecca's strength.

```
◆Current Status◆
> ARIHITO called on ARIADNE for aid
> ARIADNE summoned ALPHECCA
```

"I am Alphecca, incarnation of Arianrhod, the Silver Chariot."

Alphecca announced herself as she appeared out of thin air. With Ceres and Steiner's help, I got Alphecca connected to the chassis of our cart.

"That's as much as we can do, I'm afraid," said Ceres. "We're praying for your success, Arihito!"

"Take care, everyone…," said Steiner. "We'll be right here, waiting for your return!"

"Okay…time to fire the Queen's Tail!"

```
◆Current Status◆
> MADOKA used ★QUEEN'S TAIL +1 to activate
  STING RAY ⟶ Terrain: Rampart successfully
  destroyed
> ARIHITO activated CHARGE ASSIST 1 ⟶ MADOKA
  recovered magic
```

Light arced upward from the Queen's Tail, then fell like a meteor to pierce the stronghold wall across the river. It looked a little weaker than the test shot, due to the increased distance, but it was still strong enough to destroy the wall.

"Let's go!"

◆Current Status◆
> Ariadne converted Arihito's devotion level into magic
> Alphecca activated Endless Loop ⟶ Alphecca stopped consuming magic
> Alphecca activated Constellation ⟶ Area of skill effects increased
> Alphecca activated Floating ⟶ Obstacles and elevation have no effect

Alphecca extended the range of her skills to cover the connected cart; it rose into the air along with the Silver Chariot, and together they began to glide forward through the sky.

"A-Arihito! We're really flying! Eeek!"

"Don't worry, Madoka, you're not going to fall down. But stay on guard, Alphecca. One of the enemies we're up against can make new obstacles!"

"They have arrived. The enemy is trying to obstruct our path to the stronghold wall."

◆Current Status◆
> Simian Lord Minion: Terraformer activated Tectonic Rise ⟶ Formed Ground Pillars
> Alphecca activated Crescent Drift

> Arihito activated Hawk Eyes ⟶ Increased
  ability to monitor the situation

Alphecca used her Crescent Drift, which was typically an offensive maneuver, to avoid the Terraformer's pillars as they shot up out of the ground with frightening speed. Even as I felt dizzying g-forces on all sides, I noticed the Terraformer himself on the opposite side of the obstruction.

◆Current Status◆
> Simian Lord Minion: Terraformer activated Tectonic
  Rise ⟶ Formed Ground Pillars
> Simian Lord Minion: Terraformer activated Creeping
  Vines ⟶ Thorned Ivy grew on Ground Pillars

Suddenly, vines sprouted on the pillars, growing to connect each pillar to the next in a network of thorny vines—but Alphecca didn't slow down.

"*Such an obstacle will not stop me,*" she said.

◆Current Status◆
> Alphecca activated Thorn Rut
> Alphecca activated Perpetual Devastation

Alphecca rarely showed any major emotional shifts, but there was pride in her voice—so much pride that it verged on haughtiness. She rode about on the clinging vines as she pleased, attacking boldly and indiscriminately. I never imagined that a skill as oppressively stifling as the Terraformer's Creeping Vines could be used to provide greater mobility instead.

"Eeeek!"

"Hold on tight, everyone!"

"*I shall not let a single one of you fall. Fear not! Entrust yourselves to me!*"

Alphecca ran along the ivy, pulling our cart up an incline so steep, I thought we were on a roller coaster. It was a strange feeling to ride behind her; it felt less like we were linked to the Silver Chariot and more like we were following along with her, somehow keeping up without our cart falling through the air.

And yet there we were. Alphecca pulled us along a route the Terraformer couldn't have possibly anticipated, all the way up to the tops of the pillars, flitting about through the air. From our high vantage point, I suddenly caught sight of the Terraformer down on the ground, looking up at us.

I can see everything from up here... I can't miss!

◆Current Status◆
> ARIHITO activated VINE SHOT ⟶ Activated
  effects of SATISFACTION STONE
> Critical hit on SIMIAN LORD MINION: TERRAFORMER
SIMIAN LORD MINION: TERRAFORMER was restrained by
  Vines

"It hit... I'm pretty sure you could get away with introducing yourself as a Sniper at this point, Arihito!" said Elitia.

"I bet that Terraformer's just as surprised to get hit from this distance, too. I'd like to make sure he's all right, if possible, but from this position he looks okay..."

"Kozelka and Khosrow are still fighting... We must keep up, too!" said Seraphina.

Once we passed through the shattered wall and into the central stronghold, I could count on Hawk Eyes to let me see the lay of the land through all the obstructions. The river flowing through the labyrinth's second floor surrounded the Simian Lord's strongholds; they were built on an island in the middle of it, with flame traps set up in the rear to prevent assault from behind.

"I knew it... The Simian Lord's got Rury..."

"What in the world is that in front of it, though...?" asked Seraphina.

```
◆Monsters Encountered◆
☆SHINING SIMIAN LORD
Level Unknown
Hostile
Fire Resistant
Dropped Loot: ???
SIMIAN LORD MINION: HEALER
Level 11
Hostile
Dropped Loot: ???
SIMIAN LORD MINION: PUPPETEER
Level 13
Hostile
```

```
Dropped Loot: ???
?GIANT PUPPET
Level 10
Dropped Loot: ???
```

Before us was an enormous ape with fur like a blazing flame. Unlike the other apes we'd seen so far, this one was wearing an armored helmet that certainly made it look the part of the evil overlord. One Seeker sat on each of its shoulders: Rury and the Puppeteer that Ivril had mentioned.

Positioned right in front of it, at the very center of the central stronghold, was the thing that Seraphina had asked about: an enormous statue. Its face was wrapped in bandages, but it looked like it might start moving at any moment—and in each hand, it clutched a large, strangely shaped sword.

"Mr. Atobe!" Seraphina called.

A chill went through my body; with Hawk Eyes enhancing my vision, I saw the Simian Lord from far above.

```
◆Current Status◆
☆SHINING SIMIAN LORD activated PURGATORIAL FIREBALL
   → Target: ALPHECCA
Certain Hit
```

So it was entirely possible for a powerful enemy attack skill to have the Certain Hit effect. Faced with that, there was only one thing we could do: try to reduce the damage as much as possible. That was all.

"Seraphina, use Defense Force and Aura Shield, please!" I yelled.

"...!"

◆Current Status◆
> Ariadne activated Guard Variant ⟶ Target: Alphecca
> Seraphina activated Defense Force and Aura Shield
> Arihito activated Defense Support 2 ⟶ Support Types: Defense Force, Aura Shield
> Purgatorial Fireball hit Alphecca

"This is it... The Simian Lord's flame..."

"Alphecca!"

Even with us using all the defensive skills we could muster to reduce the damage, it still left Alphecca's chariot in bad shape. She still somehow managed to maintain the effects of her Float skill as she brought us safely to the ground.

"Alphecca, please release your manifestation for a moment! Otherwise...you might—"

"I cannot do that... If you are to use this weapon again, you will need my protection."

"I...I see... We'll buy you as much time as we can. Just please keep Madoka safe!"

Elitia, Seraphina, Theresia, and I left Alphecca and headed onward toward the Simian Lord—though we still had a lot of ground to cover before we reached it.

"GUAAGHAHA... GAGAGAGAGAGAH!"

The Simian Lord gave a belly laugh, thoroughly amused. Elitia and Seraphina came to a stop in front of the enormous statue at the center of the stronghold. Then the evil ape's booming laughter stopped—and it was as if the curtain rose to reveal a nightmare from which there was no escape.

◆Current Status◆
> Simian Lord Minion: Puppeteer activated Marionette
   ⟶ ?Giant Puppet transformed into Battle Puppet
> ☆Shining Simian Lord activated Devil's Atonement
   ⟶ Battle Puppet strengthened by underlings'
   karma ⟶ Battle Puppet transformed into
   ★Wicked Battle Puppet

Now why did the Simian Lord send its subjugated Seekers and underling monsters out instead of keeping them close by its side? There was a reason for making them fight that was unrelated to their actual combat ability. All monsters affiliated with the Simian Lord accumulated karma as they fought with Seekers, and if that was what the Simian Lord was after, it might have just attained its goal—a Battle Puppet powered up by karma. I was afraid to check my license, even though I knew what I would find on it.

◆Monster Encountered◆
★Wicked Battle Puppet
Level 15

```
Hostile
Fire Resistant
Sleep Resistant
Paralysis Resistant
Stun Resistant
Dropped Loot: ???
```

Level 15. Encountering a monster of that level in a District Five labyrinth was unthinkable, and yet the Simian Lord had successfully created one. It had been preparing for this since the moment it took a Puppeteer under its command, and all that preparation was paying off.

"Arihito..."

Elitia looked back toward me. I knew how hard it was to press onward without losing all will to fight under the circumstances; I understood that so well that it hurt. But the Puppeteer was a wall that we had no choice but to go over. On the other side of that wall, our real target—the Simian Lord—waited and watched, leisurely laughing.

"GUAGAGAGAGA...!"

```
◆Current Status◆
>  ☆SHINING SIMIAN LORD activated PURGATORIAL PRISON
   → Area effect: High Heat
>  ☆SHINING SIMIAN LORD activated WAR DRUM →
   ★WICKED BATTLE PUPPET's attack power and speed
   increased
```

```
>  ☆SHINING SIMIAN LORD activated TYRANNICAL
   OPPRESSION ──→ ARIHITO's party's morale was
   reduced by 10
```

"It's trying to cut us off from using Morale Discharges right away!"

"How much of a joke does it think we are—?!" Elitia's voice sounded strained.

The Simian Lord spread a wall of fire in front of itself, ensuring that we wouldn't be able to reach it without going through the Battle Puppet first. It was confident that the completed Battle Puppet would be able to defeat us on its own. Its level was nearly twice my own—and in a world where a gap of one level makes a difference, a seven-level gap was tremendous.

But we're gonna fill that gap! Get ready, Simian Lord—we're coming!

The Battle Puppet was protected by what appeared to be a patchwork of armor taken from Seekers. Its swords looked like they were also Seekers' weapons, or at least had been at some point. The Simian Lord's flames were likely hot enough for metalworking, then. The Puppet's two swords were coal black and enormous; one look at them told me that staving off their attacks would be next to impossible.

The Puppet's face was covered with a simian mask under a horned helmet. It may have been a coincidence, but it looked an awful lot like a feudal warlord from Japanese history. Only much, much bigger.

Suddenly, the Battle Puppet held both of its swords over its head and bent at the knee. We were already within its attack range. Common sense held that a monster as large as this one would move slowly, but that didn't apply here. The Battle Puppet's swords came swinging down in a flash.

"In the name of the Hidden Gods, I protect thee..."

◆Current Status◆
> ARIHITO activated DEFENSE SUPPORT 1 ⟶ Target: SERAPHINA
> ARIADNE activated GUARD VARIANT ⟶ Target: SERAPHINA
> ★WICKED BATTLE PUPPET used its RIGHT ARM to activate HARDEDGE STARCRUSHER
> SERAPHINA activated DEFENSE FORCE, AURA SHIELD, and GUARDIAN'S TASK
> HARDEDGE STARCRUSHER hit SERAPHINA
★MIRRORED SHELL PAVIS +1's durability was reduced

"Seraphina!"

"I can handle it...with Mr. Atobe and Ariadne's power on my side..."

My Defense Support 1 skill reduced the damage by 13 points, which was hardly a fraction of the damage headed her way. But even though the blow looked strong enough to knock her shield completely away, Seraphina withstood it. By blocking the attack, she created a gap in the onslaught to allow for a counterattack. Elitia moved to strike, but then—

Our miraculous opportunity crumbled to pieces as the Battle Puppet brought down its second sword.

It's no use! If this attack hits Seraphina head-on, we're in real trouble...!

The sword in the Battle Puppet's left hand turned from black to red hot. We were facing down a powerful fire elemental attack—one that covered too wide a range for Seraphina to hold it off herself.

"Mr. Atobe, shield everyone, now!" Seraphina called back to me.

The next moment, a transparent wall appeared directly in front of me.

"Here comes the support, guys!"

◆Current Status◆
> ARIADNE activated GUARD VARIANT ⟶ Target: ARIHITO
> SERAPHINA affixed ARIHITO with DEFENSIVE BARRIER AURA
> ARIHITO activated DEFENSE SUPPORT 2 ⟶ Support Types: DEFENSIVE BARRIER AURA, GUARD VARIANT
> ★WICKED BATTLE PUPPET used its LEFT ARM to activate HARDEDGE BLACK FLAME WHIRLWIND ⟶ Fire elemental area of effect attack
> Hit SERAPHINA
No damage

```
> Hit ELITIA
No damage
> Hit ARIHITO
> Hit THERESIA
```

"Theresia!"

"......!!"

Even though my armor was stronger than before, my defensive power was still significantly lessened when I was on the front lines. If it hadn't been for Defensive Barrier Aura and Guard Variant—not to mention Theresia protecting me with her own shield—the Battle Puppet's black flames would have mowed me down.

```
◆Current Status◆
> ★QUEEN'S TAIL +1 commenced cooldown
Capable of refiring in 718 seconds
```

We still couldn't fire the Queen's Tail, our ace in the hole. We'd fired it twice already, extending its cooldown time. It would be more than ten minutes until it was ready to fire again; it was useless if we couldn't hold out against the Battle Puppet's furious onslaught for that long.

No... Even if I focus entirely on protecting everyone, it'll still crush us before then... I've gotta go on the offensive, even just a little bit!

Theresia sprang into action as if she'd read my thoughts. I

couldn't tell her it was no use. Her every movement was deliberate, without a hint of hesitation; her target was clear.

"......!"

```
◆Current Status◆
> THERESIA activated ACCEL DASH and DOUBLE THROW
> ARIHITO activated FORCE SHOT: FREEZE
> ★WICKED BATTLE PUPPET used its RIGHT ARM to
  activate HARDEDGE DROP ⟶ Ready to counter
> ★WICKED BATTLE PUPPET used its LEFT ARM to
  activate TITANIC FALL
> THERESIA activated MIRAGE and SHADOW STEP
> FORCE SHOT: FREEZE hit ★WICKED BATTLE PUPPET
> TITANIC FALL triggered DELAYED IMPULSE
Hit THERESIA
> ★HIDE AND SEEK +5 was broken
```

Theresia's body went sailing through the air.

An invisible shock wave had followed after the Battle Puppet brought down its sword, hitting Theresia hard and sending her flying. She bounced across the ground several times and finally rolled to a stop.

My heart pounded and my vision went red. Bitter hatred swelled up inside me; it felt like I was burning up. I had to destroy the Battle Puppet; every second it still stood was a second too long.

But I knew what had happened, and my allies did, too. We knew that Theresia had charged forward to challenge the Puppet in order to help me survive, if only for a moment longer.

"I won't lose you again… I swore I wouldn't!" Elitia yelled.

◆Current Status◆
> Elitia activated Asterisk ⟶ Certain hit when
  striking weak points
Increased probability of critical hit
Unique terrain: Star Field

Elitia's eyes were no longer bloodred. Instead, a shining light poured out of them, as if they contained twinkling stars they couldn't hold inside. Her body moved of its own accord. It knew that there was only one option left to take.

◆Current Status◆
> Arihito activated Attack Support 1
> Elitia activated Comet Raid
> Terrain effect: Star Field grants Elitia
  preemptive strikes
★Wicked Battle Puppet's actions were delayed

My eyes can't keep up with Elitia…and neither can the Battle Puppet!

"Scatter, as stars fall!"

◆Current Status◆
> Elitia activated Ultimatum ⟶ Attack power
  and speed increased
Added Scarlet Trails

```
> ELITIA activated STAR PARADE ⟶ Attack
  frequency increased
> ★WICKED BATTLE PUPPET activated HARDEDGE DREAMING
  DAWN
```

The Battle Puppet attempted to counterattack, despite the effects of the Star Field holding it back.

Did you see this coming...Theresia...?

```
◆Current Status◆
> THERESIA's thrown ELLUMINATE RAZOR SWORD +7 hit
  ★WICKED BATTLE PUPPET
13 support damage
```

Even though Theresia hadn't thrown two weapons when she activated Double Throw, it still ensured that the one she did throw would hit the Battle Puppet. The Razor Sword careened down out of the sky, striking the Puppet and delaying its skill for an instant.

"Mr. Atobe...!"

"Cooperation Support...vanguards!"

```
◆Current Status◆
> ARIHITO activated COOPERATION SUPPORT 1
> ELITIA activated LIBERATION ⟶ Unlocked ANTARES
  ability: SCARLET SHADOW BLADE
> ELITIA activated LUMINOUS FLOW ⟶ 63 stages
  hit ★WICKED BATTLE PUPPET
Added 63 SCARLET TRAILS
```

```
63 weak point critical hits
Combined attack stage 1
> ELITIA activated additional attacks
42 stages hit
42 weak point critical hits
Added 42 SCARLET TRAILS
> SERAPHINA activated FANATIC ⟶ Stats increased
> SERAPHINA activated SHIELD SLAM ⟶ Hit ★WICKED
  BATTLE PUPPET
Combined attack stage 2
> Combined attack LUMINOUS SLAM ⟶ Critical
  hit on ★WICKED BATTLE PUPPET
1,378 support damage
26 additional cooperation damage
```

That's another thing Elitia's Asterisk does... It makes all attacks that hit a weak point into critical hits. It doesn't matter that the enemy's level 15... All that strength won't stop Elitia's skill from connecting!

"Blossoms of scarlet blades, bloom!"

```
◆Current Status◆
> ARIHITO activated ATTACK SUPPORT 2 ⟶ Support
  Type: FORCE SHOT: FREEZE
> ELITIA unleashed accumulated SCARLET TRAILS
Activated 105 stage slash attack
> ★WICKED BATTLE PUPPET was Frozen
★WICKED BATTLE PUPPET's actions were canceled
> SIMIAN LORD MINION: PUPPETEER linked with ★WICKED
  BATTLE PUPPET
```

```
Simian Lord Minion: Puppeteer fainted due to
    decrease in magic
>  Simian Lord Minion: Healer activated Awaken ⟶
    Simian Lord Minion: Puppeteer recovered from
    fainting
```

All of this was due to the truly miraculous number of moves that Elitia could use. By changing the target of my Attack Support before she released her Scarlet Trails, I could choose a special attack that had a chance to get through to the enemy. It was a choice between that or support damage, but considering the Puppeteer had fainted, I thought it'd be risky to deal too much damage to the Battle Puppet—since the Puppet and the Puppeteer were linked, they would share damage, too.

"…Are you just going to watch from behind those flames of yours?" Elitia called out, pointing her sword toward the Simian Lord beyond the Purgatorial Prison.

Through the flickering fire, I could see that the Simian Lord looked astonished. However…

"GUGHAAA… GUGHAHAHAHAHA!"

"It's still…laughing…!"

The Simian Lord stretched its arms out toward the eastern and western strongholds. Ariadne filled me in on what was going on there: Kozelka's and Khosrow's teams had subdued each of the Simian Lord's cohorts without incident.

I'm pretty sure we've got the Simian Lord cornered… But it looks like it's not over yet!

"Wait, it's…it's crying…?"

Between my Hawk Eyes and Elitia's Asterisk, I could see something that I typically wouldn't have been able to notice with the naked eye: tears on the Simian Lord's face. But there was no way they were tears of grief for its fallen underlings.

They were tears of joy—the joy of acquiring new power.

"GUGHAAAHHH…!!"

◆Current Status◆
> ☆Shining Simian Lord activated Demonic Soul
  Summoning ⟶ Absorbed ★Stonesplitting Savage
  Simian's and ★Demon Monkey Guard's souls
  ☆Shining Simian Lord evolved into ☆Blazing Simian
  King

"GUOOOH… GOOOHHHHHH!!"

Two orbs, gleaming black as they fluttered through the air, flew into the Simian Lord's outstretched hands. The Simian Lord swallowed them down, and then its body started to change.

"It's a damned abomination…!" Elitia rasped as four arms sprouted from the Simian Lord's back—the arms of the Stonesplitting Savage Simian and the Demon Monkey Guard.

◆Current Status◆
> ☆Blazing Simian King activated Royal Skill: Flaming
  Palm of Six Hells ⟶ Began chanting a hex

The Simian Lord's Purgatorial Fireball skill was guaranteed to hit, and now one fireball was forming in each of the Simian King's six hands.

"Mr. Atobe!" Kozelka called.

"Sorry we're late, Atobe," said Khosrow. "Wow...so that's the Simian Lord?"

The Simian King laughed. Tears still streamed down its face—but were they tears of mercy for us, the soon-to-be victims of its Royal Skill, or were they tears of delight?

It pointed two of its arms forward, and two each of the remaining four toward Kozelka's and Khosrow's teams. If one of its Purgatorial Fireballs hit any of them, the wounds it dealt would be fatal. There was no doubt about that; the fact that it had rendered Alphecca incapable of moving with one hit made it all too clear.

So then the question was, How do we defend against them? I wasn't positioned behind either Kozelka or Khosrow, and thus I couldn't use any of my usual support skills.

"Atobe!"

"Hey, Arihito! Here we are!"

"We're here to support you, Arihito!"

I heard Igarashi, Misaki, and Suzuna's voices as they rode up on Cion's back. Nayuta was with them; none of them were aware that the Simian King had started casting a spell.

"Arihito...!"

"Do allow us to help, Mr. Arihito."

This time, it was Melissa, Ivril, Viola, and Ferris. Everyone in Khosrow's team was safe and accounted for—for now. The Simian

King's flames were strong enough to change that and tear the party apart with one shot.

Which made life seem all the more precious.

"This is where it ends... We're not gonna let you get away with this any longer!"

I knew my power wasn't enough to protect everyone—but *our* power was. Together, we could overcome any threat that faced us.

"I'm counting on you, Elitia! Misaki, use Fortune Roll before Elitia gets hit!"

"Okay...got it. It's all we have left...!"

"Wait, what? Uh... 'Kay! Here goes nothing!"

```
◆Current Status◆
> ARIHITO's morale increased
Morale Discharge ready
> ELITIA activated COMET RAID
```

Elitia's move would have looked reckless to anybody, even the Simian King. But that was exactly why it was just the thing to break us out of our tight spot. I believed in Elitia, just like I believed in everyone. I believed we were strong enough to defeat the Simian King.

"GUOOOOHHHHHH!!"

```
◆Current Status◆
> ☆BLAZING SIMIAN KING activated ROYAL SKILL:
  FLAMING PALM OF SIX HELLS
> MISAKI activated FORTUNE ROLL
```

```
>  ★Brísingamen's effect was activated
Damage reduced by FIRE AND HEAT PROTECTION
```

Brísingamen, the choker that Elitia had equipped on her neck, had a small chance of activating Heat Guard when she was hit by a fire elemental attack. Once the skill was triggered, however, the choker broke. Given its exorbitant price, I knew it would keep Elitia safe in this battle—but when it was combined with my skill, that safety would expand to all of us.

"Morale Discharge... Complete Mutual Support!"

```
◆Current Status◆
> ARIHITO activated COMPLETE MUTUAL SUPPORT
Time limit: 120 seconds
> Strengthened buff effect range for
  ARIHITO's party and allied parties
> All individual buff skills applied to
  entire party and allied party members
> ROYAL SKILL: FLAMING PALM OF SIX HELLS was
  nullified
```

The Simian King didn't fight alongside its underlings. Instead, it used them as doubles—and in the end, it consumed their souls to gain greater power. But here's what I thought: *If only the Simian King had joined in instead of watching as we fought the Battle Puppet... If only it had seen the monsters under its command as more than pawns on a chessboard...* It would have been nearly impossible for us to win.

"Arihito, now...!" cried Elitia.

"Right... Here goes!"

We poured all of the fighting strength we had left into our next attack. Igarashi and Melissa shifted their grips on Ambivalenz and the Forbidden Scythe, respectively, preparing for the most destructive combination they could muster.

"Cooperation Support—All Out Assault!"

◆Current Status◆
> ARIHITO activated COOPERATION SUPPORT 1 and ATTACK SUPPORT 1
> ELITIA activated STAR PARADE ⟶ Attack frequency increased
> ELITIA activated LUMINOUS FLOW ⟶ 63 stages hit ☆BLAZING SIMIAN KING
Added 63 SCARLET TRAILS
63 weak point critical hits
Combined attack stage 1
> ELITIA activated additional attacks
42 stages hit
42 weak point critical hits
Added 42 SCARLET TRAILS
> KOZELKA activated SWORD RAIN ⟶ 12 stages hit ☆BLAZING SIMIAN KING
Combined attack stage 2
> KHOSROW activated DRAGON DROP ⟶ Hit ☆BLAZING SIMIAN KING
Paralysis has no effect
Stun has no effect
Actions delayed
Combined attack stage 3

"GWOHHH... OOOOOOHHH!!"

Elitia made slash after slash faster than the eye could see, while Kozelka's blades rained down on the Simian King like a meteor shower. On top of that, Khosrow was a whirlwind of fists as he pummeled the monster.

"The Delay effect got through... Come on, we can link up more attacks!"

```
◆Current Status◆
> IVRIL activated PARASOL VORTEX ⟶ 14 stages
  hit ☆BLAZING SIMIAN KING
Combined attack stage 4
> VIOLA activated CRUEL PAIN ⟶ 6 stages hit
  ☆BLAZING SIMIAN KING
Paralysis has no effect
Bind has no effect
Combined attack stage 5
> FERESIA activated WILD LEOPARD ⟶ 8 stages hit
  ☆BLAZING SIMIAN KING
Concussion has no effect
Combined attack stage 6
> KYOUKA activated DOUBLE ATTACK ⟶ 2 stages hit
  ☆BLAZING SIMIAN KING
A portion of the damage pierced ☆BLAZING
  SIMIAN KING's defense
Combined attack stage 7
> MELISSA activated LOP OFF ⟶ ☆BLAZING SIMIAN
  KING dropped materials
Critical hit
```

```
Instant Death has no effect
Combined attack stage 8
Reached combined attack limit
> Combined attack LUMINOUS SWORD DRAGON DROP:
  VORTEX LASHING LEOPARD SLICE → 1,937 support
  damage
104 additional cooperation damage
```

Ivril let her spinning parasol fly off to shave away at the Simian King, while Viola battered it with a flurry of whip lashes. Ferris rushed into the fray and struck so quickly and repeatedly that she looked like a blur. Igarashi let loose two attacks that sharply knocked the Simian King's head down, and Melissa took the opportunity to lop off one of the horns on its head with the Forbidden Scythe.

"It's working…," said Khosrow. "Our attacks aren't just connecting, they're building up real damage! Pretty nice trick you got there, Arihito."

He was right. Between their powerful skills themselves and the nearly two thousand points of support damage added on, it looked like we were seriously hurting the Simian King. There was just one problem: It still had a healer sitting on its shoulder—Rury. That meant that, unless we killed the Simian King outright, it could recover from any damage.

I had no way of knowing that it would work, but I figured that if we could somehow poke a hole in its resistances, we had a decent chance of winning.

"Suzuna, play your flute... It's got the Silent Stone!"

Suzuna didn't waste time answering; she started playing the flute immediately. The Silent Stone gave it a different timbre than it had with the stagnation stone.

```
◆Current Status◆
> Suzuna activated Sound of Silence
> Simian Lord Minion: Healer fell silent
> No effect on ☆Blazing Simian King
> No effect on Simian Lord Minion: Puppeteer
> Simian Lord Minion: Healer activated Heal Wound
  → Activation failed
```

We stopped her from healing it... Without perfect resistances, our status ailments should get through!

"Just a little more... But how's Theresia?!"

Right—Theresia had to deal the final blow. But she wasn't in any condition to stand and fight, even if Recovery Support would help. And meanwhile, though the Simian King was bleeding all over, it still refused to kneel. The sinister atmosphere hadn't lifted.

"Woof...!!"

Cion took notice and ran as fast as the wind to help the fallen Theresia.

A memory of our first battle with the Simian Lord flashed in my mind. In that memory, I saw that the monster had another weapon: the giant chain wrapped around its body.

"GHAAAAAAH!!"

◆Current Status◆
> ☆Blazing Simian King activated Concealed Weapon
Cast
> Cion activated Emergency Extraction

Even assuming Cion reached her mark in time, she would be wrapped up in the chain along with Theresia. As weakened as Theresia was, being restrained in and of itself would be too much for her.

We should have saved her earlier... Wait, no... There's still time!

"You would do well not to forget us. Allow me to sever these bonds once again!"

"Stellar Sword, activate! Arms Device Limiter, release!"

◆Current Status◆
> Ariadne summoned Guard Arm
> Ariadne used Murakumo to activate Blade of Heaven
and Earth: Steel Slice
> Blade of Heaven and Earth: Steel Slice hit
Purgatorial Shackles ⟶ Destroyed Purgatorial
Shackles

Murakumo and Ariadne cut away the memory that struck fear into Alphecca. The Simian King jeered at us as it began to heave its chain; the glee drained from its face before the chain left its hand. At that moment, the Simian King looked desperate to survive.

◆Current Status◆
> ☆Blazing Simian King restrained Simian Lord
  Minion: Healer and Simian Lord Minion: Puppeteer
> ☆Blazing Simian King began charging Flash of
  Devastation

With two of its arms, the Simian King grabbed hold of Rury and the Puppeteer to use them as a shield. This prevented us from attacking while it began to gather their magic power into its forehead.

We were powerless to fight back. One of us had to take the Simian King's attack—and I didn't need to know the specifics to understand that whoever Flash of Devastation hit, the result would be the same: death.

"This is it... This is my time...!"

◆Current Status◆
> Seraphina activated Provoke ⟶ Increased
  ☆Blazing Simian King's hostility toward
  Seraphina

"Seraphina...!"

"I'll take the blow... So please, Mr. Atobe, make sure Theresia gets there!"

Seraphina meant to sacrifice herself to give Theresia a chance to counterattack. But I didn't want to lose Seraphina. There had to be something I could do—but what?

"Fear not, devotee...for I shall protect you without fail."

◆Current Status◆
> Ariadne summoned Fylgja
> Fylgja activated Armor Change ⟶ Fylgja powered
  up Seraphina's ★Altered Glacial Plate +1
> Seraphina activated Aura Shield
> Fylgja activated Construct ⟶ Defensive power
  of each defensive skill increased

"I am Fylgja. Don the armor of a Hidden God, devotee; I shall protect you."

Fylgja's voice resounded as Seraphina's armor changed shape.

The Simian King was smiling again, confident that it could kill Seraphina. The magic that it gathered in its forehead burst outward in an explosion of light. But at that moment...

"Runes, grant me strength... *Alternate Body*!"

"Everyone gets out alive... Everyone!" Misaki cried.

◆Current Status◆
> Seraphina activated Alternate Body ⟶ Maximum
  vitality increased by half of magic power
> ☆Blazing Simian King activated Flash of
  Devastation ⟶ Hit Seraphina
> Misaki activated Pool Cap ⟶ Reduced damage
  to Seraphina to avert death
Misaki fainted

Seraphina blocked the Flash of Devastation with her Mirrored Shell Pavis. Even with the combined defensive power of Fylgja and the Altered Glacial Plate, Seraphina likely wouldn't have survived if it hadn't been for the Alter Rune effects and Misaki's Pool Cap.

"Hyaaah… I'm toast…"

"Misaki…!"

The Simian King had tried to claim at least one of my companions and take them over to its side. But it wasn't getting its way. While Seraphina intercepted the Flash of Devastation, I made my way over to Theresia's side.

"……"

The hex marked on the back of Theresia's neck was spreading. She could no longer move.

I'm still going to save you, Theresia… I swear I will!

I knew I'd gained another level the moment we defeated the Battle Puppet.

"Theresia…let's do it together. I know we can!"

"……!"

I propped Theresia up and held her upright. With great difficulty, she managed to stand on her own two feet and hold the Gloria Stiletto in a backhanded grip.

"GIIIGIIGII… GYAGYAHHH!"

The Simian King snickered, as if the moment it'd been waiting for had finally arrived.

"……!!"

◆Current Status◆
> ☆Blazing Simian King activated Incite Treachery
   → Target: Theresia

The Simian King played the very last card in its hand: attempting to take control of Theresia as the hex consumed her. If Theresia turned hostile, we'd have no way to land a single hit with a Curse Eater weapon. Without that, Theresia would never be free of the hex, even with the Simian King dead.

"GHUGAGA... GHAAAGAGAGA...!"

"Theresia...!" Elitia cried out.

She could have unleashed her Scarlet Trails and destroyed the Simian King—but she didn't. Instead, she strode up and stood in front of the monster, completely defenseless.

The Simian King reached a hand toward Elitia, ready to unleash its purgatorial flames. We'd fought so hard to get into a winning position, but a direct hit at such close range would completely turn the tables.

But then...

"...GHHH... GHAHA..."

The Simian King's confidence melted away along with its ferocious grin.

"—!"

◆Current Status◆
> THERESIA'S PSYCHE BARRIER 1 activated
> PSYCHE BARRIER 1's success ensured by
  THERESIA'S and party members' Trust Levels
> INCITE TREACHERY was nullified
PSYCHE BARRIER 1 deactivated

The Psyche Barrier Lynée had deployed pulled Theresia back from the brink of ruin.

"GAH... GHAAAHHH!"

Elitia turned back our way. The Simian King panicked, pushing forward its hostages as if to parade them in front of us. We were watching the last moments of this monster, who had caused such long, horrible suffering for so many Seekers.

"Theresia... Elitia... I've got your backs!"

```
◆Current Status◆
> ARIHITO learned ☆◆xo✳3 ⟶ Skill identified
  as ATTACK SUPPORT 3
> ARIHITO activated ATTACK SUPPORT 3 ⟶ Support
  Type: THERESIA's attacks
Target: ELITIA
```

"GUWOOOAAAHHH!!"

The Simian King spit its last vicious roar at us—but that was no longer enough to scare me and my friends.

"You've underestimated humans for the last time, Your Royal Monkeyness."

```
◆Current Status◆
> ELITIA unleashed accumulated SCARLET TRAILS
Activated 105 stage attack
> THERESIA's attacks hit 105 times due to
  ATTACK SUPPORT 3
Critical hit
> Defeated 1 ☆BLAZING SIMIAN KING
Activated CURSE EATER
```

> ☆BLAZING SIMIAN KING'S SEALS OF SUBORDINATION
  vanished

Elitia sheathed her sword. She unleashed her Scarlet Trails one after the other, with enough time between them for Theresia to strike along with each of them with the Gloria Stiletto. The cornered Simian King took the full force of the assault. In its desperation to survive, it had used every trick at its disposal. Creating the Battle Puppet, trapping Seekers in the Blazing Red Mansion—maybe all of that had been for the sake of survival. But what was it hoping to find when it outlived everything? What was its goal then?

I might never find out. The only thing that mattered in that moment was that we'd won. All I wanted to do was rejoice that Theresia, Rury, and the rest of the Seekers were free from the beast's clutches.

"Rury!"

The subjugated Seekers pitched forward and fell face-first from the Simian King's enfeebled arms. Cion rushed in to catch the Puppeteer in the nick of time, while Elitia grabbed Rury.

"Rury... Rury... Please, Rury, wake up...!"

Elitia pleaded with her friend as the rest of us stood by watching. Tears fell from her eyes.

"...Ellie...," came the sound of Rury's voice at last.

"Ah... Ohhh..."

She was safe. I breathed a sigh of relief as my chest swelled with emotion.

"...Thank you...for working so hard to save me...all this time..."

"O-of course... I...I just couldn't take losing you... All along, I just wanted...to talk to you again..."

Back when I first met Elitia in District Eight and heard of her quest to rescue Rury, it almost felt as if that day would never come. Other Seekers shunned Elitia and called her names, but she kept fighting, even though she fought alone. All her heroic resolve, all her effort and devotion, had finally been rewarded.

"......"

"Everything's going to be all right, Theresia. The hex is gone... I'm so glad."

Theresia clung to my arm and looked up at me. Beneath the lizard mask, her mouth curved up into a smile.

We'd fought to win back people who were precious to us—and we'd won. There was no way I could ever thank everyone who'd fought alongside me and everyone who'd pitched in to support us enough.

Igarashi wiped tears from her eyes. Misaki and Suzuna, too; Misaki was still a little woozy from using Pool Cap, but she'd at least recovered enough to stand up again.

Kozelka and Khosrow smiled at me. Even Ceres and her crew had made it all the way into the central stronghold—after seeing how greatly the tide of battle had changed, I assumed.

"Arihito... I am glad to see you made it through the fight without any casualties."

"Yeah… Thanks to you, Ariadne, Murakumo, Alphecca, Fylgja—and everyone else."

If any one of us hadn't been there, I doubt we would've been so successful.

Thus ended our long struggle against the Simian Lord. The only thing left to do for the time being was to share in the joy of victory.

EPILOGUE

While the battle raged on, Ceres and her crew tried following Arihito into the Simian Lord's stronghold only to meet with some trouble. Arihito told them to sit tight and wait in place because they all played support roles—but despite that, he also knew that he could use all the strength he could get from those who'd joined him in the labyrinth.

"Tch... It looks like we've all ended up charmed by Arihito. I've got to wonder just how far I'd have gone if I'd met him when I was still an active Seeker," said Luca.

The Simian Lord's abilities prevented the Familiar Arrow from offering Luca and the rest a clear view of what was going on in the strongholds. All they had to go on was the clamor of battle. Amid the sounds and the screams, the four of them laid bare their own feelings from combat experiences long past.

"Believe you me, I'm perfectly happy to support 'em as much as I can like this," said Ceres. "When Arihito and crew first stumbled into my workshop, they couldn't even manage a rough sketch of how they were gonna get this far. In spite of it all, I can't help but think it was fate that brought 'em to me, and fate that brought us here... Defies belief, doesn't it?"

"Um... When Commander Seraphina introduced me to Mr. Atobe, we didn't say much... I still haven't been able to talk to him much, actually," said Adeline. "But then the commander stepped away from the Guild Saviors and joined his party, and I followed along... It wasn't an easy fight, but I was just so glad to be involved, even for a little bit. And I know it'll keep up—I don't doubt it for a second! I know that sounds silly, though, since I can't really do much to help."

Ceres grinned back at Adeline. "I know exactly how you feel," that grin seemed to say. There was no need to put it into words.

"*Compared to those who actually fight monsters, we supporters play a very small part,*" Steiner added. "*But when they need us, even playing a small part feels good. And then that happiness turns into a different feeling—like, motivation to do even better, or to make them even happier.*"

"In that case," said Ceres, "it seems like all of us here, plus Falma and the other supporters, are wrapped up in a shared destiny."

"Look at me," said Luca. "I never dreamed I'd end up working for one patron exclusively! I always thought I was master of my own domain when I was working freelance, but now? Why, I feel like an apprentice tailor all over again!"

"Right... I wonder how Arihito and his crew are putting the stuff we made for 'em to use. It's that feeling, that wait for results, that takes me back to how I felt when I first started practicing my craft— Hm?!"

Ceres and the rest of the group all felt it: Someone was calling on their power. At that exact moment, Arihito had activated Complete Mutual Support, which used the effects of their support to reinforce the entire party.

"...My Haute Couture skill augments the effects of armor... I never thought I'd see the day the skill itself would power up another person, but Arihito's doing exactly that."

"Is that what's going on here? I wonder if he's making use of my Hunter skills, too..."

"I think Mr. Atobe's always been one of those people who like helping others. But that on its own doesn't explain it... It feels like it's written in the stars."

"That's an awful romantic notion for a bucket of bolts, but I think you're onto something."

The four of them turned toward the source of this new voice to see Lynée and Schwarz approaching. There was a third person with them, too: a woman with purple hair.

"What in the world is a Guide doing in a place like this...?" asked Ceres.

"I happened to run into Lynée on my way here. For some reason, I just had to see what Arihito was up to with my own eyes. Ah—please call me Yukari for now, by the way. That's the name Arihito knows me by."

"A Guide...," said Luca. "You're not the one I met when I was a fresh face in the Labyrinth Country. I suppose they assigned you to Arihito, then?"

"Let's see... I can't get into the details with you supporters, I'm afraid, but I've taken a special interest in Arihito's doings. You might say I'm a fan of his."

Yukari's mysterious air put Ceres and the others at a loss. They weren't sure exactly how they were meant to feel about her. Was Yukari friend or foe? Ceres, at least, couldn't say for sure. Either way, Yukari faced the stronghold, looking concerned for Arihito and his party.

"Honestly, I wish they'd waited to fight the Simian Lord after they'd become a little bit stronger...but they rarely do things the way I'd wish. Then again, that's what makes them so interesting."

"A Guide taking that kind of interest in a specific Seeker? Can't say I expect that to end well," said Ceres.

"Hee-hee... Is it really any different from a jade working for one? At least for the time being, I don't have any ill intent for Arihito and his party. Merely expectations."

"You do realize Arihito left us to wait here himself, right? So what's all this about his *doings*? They're off fighting for their friends right now. If you mean to butt in like it's some sort of game, then we're not going to let you do it—Guide or not."

"If you have any opinions to share with me, at least turn that vague form of yours back to normal before you spout them. Well, Ceres?"

"..."

Ceres looked to be somewhere in the vicinity of ten years old, but in truth, she was much, much older. Yukari had seen through the illusion with a glance. Ceres was instantly struck by the strangeness of this purple-haired woman and took a step back in surprise.

"I'll leave Arihito in your hands, then. I didn't come here to threaten you. But I will tell you one thing: The White Night Brigade has made their way into this labyrinth."

"What...?!" Ceres cried.

"They aren't here in full force," Yukari continued. "Only a few members. I do hope this doesn't end up splintering the Brigade... It wouldn't be any fun if Arihito's party finally mustered enough fighting strength just for the Brigade to wind up weaker, now would it?"

"It sounds like you're trying to turn Seekers against each other... Can't say that strikes me as a wholesome hobby," said Ceres.

"I agree," Luca chimed in. "What is this to you, a test for Arihito's party? They're fighting for their lives in there. If you're planning on getting in their way, then I'm afraid it's no more Mr. Nice Tailor."

"Oh, Luca," said Yukari, "and here I was, thinking so highly of your work after you made such a dashing suit for Arihito... That's right, I know that much. I also know why little Chiara wears that armor and why Adeline here joined the Guild Saviors, too."

She looked each one of the four supporters in the face before turning back toward the stronghold; her eyes grew slightly wider.

The ground itself shook. Adeline was the first to understand what that meant.

"We couldn't see into the central stronghold before, but we can now... The Simian Lord, it's...!"

"So you pulled it off, eh, Arihito? And Elitia...and all the rest."

"Well, I don't want to intrude on the celebrations, so I'll see myself out. Tell Arihito I was here, or don't. That's up to you to decide... Oh, right." Yukari started to leave, but stopped and turned back toward to Ceres as if she'd just remembered something. "Isn't it about time the party had a proper name? Considering that they've just felled the Simian Lord, they're about to gain a reputation in District Five for outdoing the White Night Brigade."

"...I'll give them the message. I'd prefer not to keep any secrets for now. Makes for a much more pleasant conversation," said Ceres.

"How amusing. I'll be praying that the rest of you keep things interesting for me from now on, too."

"Treating people like your personal clowns is not exactly a good look, you know."

"Well, I'm certainly no match for you when it comes to good looks, Luca. There. Aren't those such kind parting words? I'll see you all later."

With that, Yukari walked off. Before she'd made it very far, Ceres blinked—and when she opened her eyes again, Yukari was completely gone.

"It looks like Arihito and his friends have attracted some... potentially dangerous attention," Luca commented.

"You can say that again," said Ceres, "but she won't get her hands on them as long as I'm still around."

"That makes two of us," agreed Lynée. Now you and I have something to talk about, and I still owe Arihito and the others anyway."

"Um…," Adeline began. "S-speaking of Mr. Atobe, shouldn't we be heading over to him now? Quickly, preferably…"

"Will you be riding on my shoulder, Master?"

"Mm-hmm, if you would, Steiner."

Ceres and the rest took off running. Their licenses verified that Arihito's party had defeated the Simian King, the evolved form of the Simian Lord…and that Theresia, Rury, and the other Seekers who'd fallen under the monster's control had been freed at last.

"I wonder if Mr. Atobe's party has any ideas for a name already…," Steiner mused.

"We'll ask them about it later, seeing as whatever they pick, we'll be working under that banner, too."

In all the years since the Simian Lord had appeared on the second floor of the Blazing Red Mansion, no parties had managed to defeat it. Seeker after Seeker had tried, but it had trounced them all. The news that someone had taken it down shook District Five.

And not just any someone: a party led by the Suit Guy, and with the Death Sword herself among its members, had killed the Simian Lord. The news spread in whispers and rumors at first, but then the Guild itself made a direct announcement—in order to restore Elitia's good name.

Finally. Elitia Centrale was free from her curse and would no longer attack indiscriminately—and her new party had a name, too. Arihito and the rest made the formal proclamation.

The party that had defeated the Simian King and freed the Seekers from its domination was now called the Arianrhod.

A Ladies' Agreement Before Battle

It was the night when Theresia was allowed out of her restraints and returned to the inn from the Guild Saviors headquarters. Once morning came, Arihito's party would be heading back to the Blazing Red Mansion; the thought of it kept Kyouka and the rest of the ladies from sleeping a wink.

Kozelka was supposed to keep Theresia under her watchful eye, but instead she'd released her into Arihito's custody. Why, exactly, was a subject of some disagreement among Kyouka and her fellow party members, but they'd arrived at more or less the same general conclusion.

"It figures that Arihito would be...well, not to be too vague about it...*special* to Theresia."

"Huh? C'mon, Kyouka! You gotta spit it out directly!" said Misaki. "I mean, are you *trying* to make us all blush here?"

Madoka, Louisa, and Falma were staying in a separate room, leaving Kyouka, Misaki, Suzuna, Melissa, Seraphina, and Elitia together. The six of them were seated in pairs among the room's three beds.

Misaki was the first to venture into the living room to check on Arihito and Theresia as they rested there—and what did she see but Arihito with his arms around Theresia, stripped of her usual garb? Suzuna, who'd tagged along right behind Misaki, could hardly bring herself to speak about what she'd seen.

"Suzuna, when you say Arihito was *holding* her, you don't mean...?"

"...N-no, I don't... Well... Theresia looked like she might have meant to...but Arihito was...just too kind..."

"You don't say... Considering how Theresia must feel, I'm a little sorry for her," said Seraphina. "Mr. Atobe isn't considering the possibility we might lose to the Simian Lord tomorrow... So from that perspective..."

"No need to overcomplicate it. Surely Arihito just figured that, given how Theresia is now...a hug would be the best way to calm her down. I think he sees himself as like a big brother to us," said Melissa. She usually didn't show much interest in such topics, which made the others all the more impressed by her words.

Misaki wrapped her arms around herself as she spoke. "I know this is, like, super-wrong to say, but if I were in Theresia's shoes, d'you think there'd be a big, brotherly hug with my name on it? ...Sorry. Man, getting jealous at a time like this... I'm totally the worst..."

"Don't beat yourself up. Look, we may both wield swords, but I'm a swordfighter, and Theresia is a Rogue. If I were a Rogue like her, I'd probably want to be closer to Arihito, too... I've thought as much before myself. That's all."

"You too, Ellie? Um... I—I mean... I didn't hear anything too clearly, but..."

Suzuna started to speak, inspired by what Elitia had said, but quickly fell speechless again. Elitia didn't turn to face her, but she flushed red all the way to her ears, making her embarrassment plain to see even in profile.

"I wasn't clearly aware of it myself until recently...but I've started to see Arihito in a special light."

The other five ladies could tell just how much Elitia had to steel herself to say those words in front of them. Even Melissa, whose face rarely showed much emotion, was blushing; she understood exactly what Elitia meant.

"I want to save Theresia, Rury, and everyone else that the Simian Lord captured. And I want just as badly to keep seeking... To keep traveling the Labyrinth Country with all of you. Arihito's here, and so is everyone else. That's as precious to me as life itself nowadays."

Elitia gazed downward as she spoke, but toward the end, she lifted her head up and looked each of the five ladies in the eye, one at a time. Each and every one of them smiled back at her; Suzuna and Misaki wiped tears from their cheeks.

"I figured that, even if we all sort of knew, putting it out in the open like that would cause more of a shake-up...but it looks like I was wrong."

"Ms. Kyouka...did you feel like this about Mr. Atobe...before you came to the Labyrinth Country?"

Kyouka didn't make any effort to avoid Seraphina's abrupt question.

"I was Atobe's boss…and I thought that relationship would never change between us. I've never been able to tell him, not even once. From the moment I first saw an entry he'd made to a company-wide competition, I knew I wanted to work with him. And it's thanks to him joining my team that I managed to be a section head. I wasn't really suited for it. Whenever work wasn't going well for me, it landed on him, and I'm sure that hurt. I wish I could apologize for that… I try to fight to keep Atobe safe, but he always sees exactly what's going on and tells me not to push myself too hard. I'm awful, aren't I?"

"I see… Just as I thought, Mr. Atobe has always been kind, then. And there's nothing to say beyond that, other than that he's serious to the point that it borders on obliviousness."

Seraphina stood from her side of her bed and gave Kyouka a hug.

"…I…I've been nothing but awful to Atobe. I have no right to say he's oblivious…"

"No, that's not true."

"Huh? L-Louisa? Falma? I thought you were already asleep…"

Kyouka and the others blinked as Louisa stepped in, reassuring Kyouka as she entered. Falma was right beside her in the negligee she slept in, grinning over crossed arms.

"Ahhh, so nice to talk romance with the girls, isn't it? Brings back memories of my own seeking days."

"You ended up marrying one of the other Seekers in your party, right, Falma?"

"I sure did. My husband is still a Seeker, actually. The kids and I stick around and run the shop in District Eight to be near my mother...but I suppose labyrinths just call out to men! I've never hoped he'd retire or anything, but I do get lonely sometimes."

"U-um...I'm not sure if I should even ask this, but...don't you ever think Ari-poo is pretty adorable?"

"That would hardly be polite to say about a man older than myself! Then again, he is from...Japan, was it? People from that country always look younger than they actually are to me," said Falma, trying to avoid the question and hoping Misaki wouldn't notice she hadn't answered. But then someone jumped in with an even more pointed comment...

"I can't believe you manage to raise two children *and* run the shop while your husband is out, all while supporting us, too... I really admire you, Falma."

"Oh my, well... I'm very proud that you say so. But really, I'd say all of us supporters entrust you active Seekers with our dreams, in a way. Think of it that way—and don't hesitate to call on me if there's anything I can do for any of you from now on, too. Eyck and Plum are so mature, and every time they hear your stories of adventure, they go off about how they want to be great Seekers someday, too. As their mother, I'd prefer they stuck to something a little less dangerous, but I can't stand in the way of their dreams."

The reminder of Falma's children, Eyck and Plum, spurred

Kyouka and the others to reminisce about their own days in District Eight.

"Even if Theresia *is* the most important one of us to Ari-poo...I still wanna become the kinda person he can't do without— mmph!... Fuh...Falma, careful where you swing those weapons! B-booby violence!"

"There, there. What's the harm in being a little selfish from time to time? Mr. Atobe brought you all together by hiring you, after all. You don't need to compare his importance to you with your friendship with Theresia. Don't you agree?"

Falma spoke calmly and with reason, like a schoolteacher; even Louisa was impressed and listened raptly. In fact, Falma had even made an impression on Seraphina, who was always calm and collected.

"...Love and romance blossomed in my old party, too. When one of my comrades married a supporter, it made me think carefully about my own future. I chose the Guild Saviors...but I think that, when this party is finished in District Five, I'd like to come along. If I can, I want to travel the Labyrinth Country and put my strength to the test..."

"Is...is that right? If you ask to join us, we certainly wouldn't turn you down..."

Seraphina started out just touching on her own past, however lightly, but ended up declaring her intent for the future. At this surprising turn, the ladies of the party looked around the room from face to face, waiting to see who would speak up next.

"Ever since I met Arihito, I've been able to be truer to myself. I always used to think walking the path that was set out for me was the right thing to do. But now, I'm going to keep fighting along with Arihito and all of you—because it's what I really want to do."

"Geez, Suzu, you're always, like, so composed, even when it's girl-talk time! But I get it. I never really had anything going for me—nothing to be proud of. I mean, I even chose my Gambler job half out of desperation…but these days, I'm glad I did, 'cause I found a role in Ari-poo's party that nobody but me can play."

Suzuna and Misaki took turns sharing what Arihito meant to them. Hearing all that, Melissa piped up, though her face remained as unmoving and expressionless as ever.

"I like dissecting monsters. I know that grossed Arihito out a bit at first, but he was never mean about it. That's why I want to keep working for him."

"Ah-ha-ha… I figured you wouldn't be interested in this kinda thing, Melissa, but you really tell it like it is, huh? I totally wanna keep working for Ari-poo, too! As weird as it is for someone who used to be a total queen bee to say that."

"Well, then… It looks like it's settled. It's important for us all to respect each other's feelings about Mr. Atobe. Granted, we settled that while he's sleeping… But anyway, just that isn't enough. We also need to work harder to make him understand those feelings, even if we can't say them directly."

"Falma, could you be more specific…? No, never mind, that's up to us to figure out. Granted, even thinking about it hardly seems prudent, given my position as a Receptionist…"

"What are you talking about, Louisa? Didn't you pick a fight with me over who was going to pour wine for Atobe before? Maybe you drank so much you erased the memory, but I still remember."

"You promised not to say that! There are certain things you just can't say until you're that drunk, and besides, I had a lot of steam to blow off from work… N-no, you're right, it wasn't exactly ladylike…"

With Louisa's comments, everyone in the room began probing each other yet again; it was Kyouka who overturned the strange atmosphere.

"I totally understand how everyone feels. It looks like we're all struggling with the same problem, huh?"

"It's fair to say we're a whole party of young women…with one man among us. Personally, I respect Mr. Atobe for not getting carried away in that position."

Misaki sighed. "Don't you wonder, though? Like, are Theresia and Ari-poo, y'know…doing you-know-what?"

"I—I mean, I don't hear any v-voices… That must mean they're just resting together, right…?"

Suzuna sounded like she was about to faint. Misaki grabbed her friend to keep her upright—out of respect for how much courage it had taken her to offer her opinion in the first place—and then crept into the hall. She inched close to the living room.

"H-hey, Misaki, you can't—!"

"…Aha, I thought you weren't worried!"

"Huh…?"

Misaki and Kyouka peeped out through the cracked door and into the living room. They saw Theresia sitting awake on the sofa with Arihito's head in her lap. She glanced toward Misaki and Kyouka; in the dim light, it looked like she was smiling.

"...That's big wife energy if I ever saw it," said Misaki. "Tch, there goes Theresia showing off..."

"Well...I'm glad. I'd like to think we're not getting in their way."

"Ohhh, is *that* what that smile meant? I dunno, though..."

"Poor Atobe's such a serious guy, she's probably put him in a jam. Either way, it doesn't change how important he is to us... Tell you what, Misaki—why don't we come to an agreement?"

"I was just thinking the same thing myself. Later we can get Theresia in on it, too... Wait, though—isn't that kinda unfair?"

"Good point... But this isn't Japan, it's the Labyrinth Country. Keeping ourselves bound to what was common sense back home will probably put us in a tight spot later."

"...You're such a grown-up, Kyouka. I just can't quite make a clean break from it like that yet, y'know."

"Wh-who's making a clean break...? Look, it's one thing while Atobe is asleep, but we can't keep all this a secret forever. That wouldn't be sincere."

"Can't we just keep it up for a little longer? Sure, Theresia may be in a special spot, but if I were Ari-poo, I'd want to take good care of her, too."

The two of them returned to the ladies' bedroom to find Elitia, Suzuna, and even Seraphina waiting for them, with expressions that begged to hear what they'd discovered. Louisa and Falma had cooled off, too. Melissa's face showed that she didn't look very concerned—or it would have, if it weren't for the fact that her cheeks were bright red.

"There's something I want to discuss with you all. If we get through the battle tomorrow safe and sound..."

Now, what was Kyouka's idea? And how did the other ladies receive her suggestion? That's something Arihito wouldn't find out until a bit later...

AFTERWORD

Thank you very much for picking up Volume 8 of *The World's Strongest Rearguard*. First and foremost, I'd like to apologize for taking up so much of your time! This series has only come as far as it has thanks to the support of readers like you. Thanks again for reading.

And now a warning: Some of this afterword assumes you've already read the main story thus far, so if you skipped ahead, please go back and finish the novel before continuing!

Volume 8 represents an important waypoint on Arihito and crew's overall storyline. When Elitia joined Arihito's party back in Volume 1, she brought with her a score that had to be settled in District Five. Now that goal has been reached, and the story proceeds to its next phase.

You might be wondering, What kind of person is Rury? Will she join Arihito's party, too? And what about Johan and his White Night Brigade? Will they be an obstacle to Arihito and friends now that they've been overtaken as the top party in District Five? The Simian Lord might be gone, but Arihito's adventure in the Labyrinth Country—with all its powerful monsters and dangerous labyrinths, all its people and their comings and goings—will continue.

I imagine you've got a few different guesses as to what's in store, including a possible return to District Six. As a writer, though, my goal remains to present the story as an accumulation of choices that the party makes, one by one. The most up-to-the-minute developments in the story are currently being serialized on the web platform *Shousetsuka ni Narou*. (I think most of you are probably already aware of this, but just so you know.) I post updates every Saturday, so if you're curious and have some time to spare, I'd appreciate it if you checked it out!

If there's one thing I reflected on as I wrote the parts that would become Volume 8, it was the way monsters are named. Both readers and proofreaders asked if I would give names to the Slow Salamanders! At first I figured I would save that for a scene at the monster ranch, but since names are so important, I had to consider that perhaps Arihito should name them as soon as they join the party. At the same time, I was moved—I was delighted that people thought the Slow Salamanders needed names. What's so moving about that, you ask? Well, it felt like the Slow Salamanders were important enough to people to deserve them! They're basically gentle giants, like the Japanese giant salamander; they've got a certain charm to them, and they might even make surprisingly adorable pets. Their names are Sula and Manda. As for who decided to name them in the story itself, you'll just have to wait and read that scene.

There's another new monster at the ranch, too: the Lamia of the Deep. But if I tell you too much about her now, I think it'll spoil some of the fun. Please keep reading *The World's Strongest Rearguard* to find out about her!

There were sixteen characters who took on the Simian Lord in this volume, not counting the group of supporters that remained on standby. To tell the truth, up until I was actually writing that part of the story, there was a possibility that there'd be even more! I thought I might have Leonard and Natalia's party lend a hand. However, since facing the Simian Lord is risky business, they didn't end up fighting alongside Arihito and crew. Theirs was a chance encounter. Arihito's party will likely fight together with several other parties going forward, but at least some of these will probably just be one-time alliances.

When you factor in the support staff, Arihito's party has grown rather large, but I'd still like to write situations for everyone in it to shine.

All right, now I'd like to move on to more thank-yous!

As a writer, I bow down to the tireless efforts of my editors, who make it possible for this and every other volume of *The World's Strongest Rearguard* to see print. (I bow so deeply, in fact, that my head is basically underground at this point.) Of all the ways I could possibly show that appreciation, the one to prioritize is getting my drafts done and submitted as soon as I possibly can. From now on, I hope to move forward in earnest, without getting too bogged down in details. I promise I won't spend months on end fretting over what to call certain skills and jobs in the Labyrinth Country anymore.

Huuka Kazabana, who brings the world of *Rearguard* to life with lovely illustrations, really outdid themselves this time. Their pictures shine so brightly, I thought they'd put my eyes out. Their art is always brilliant, but their piece for the cover of Volume 8 in particular overturns preconceived notions of what it means to be a rearguard as Arihito steps forward through the composition. I think it wonderfully conveys both the contents of this volume and the relationship between Arihito and Theresia. What do you think, readers? I sincerely hope to hear your impressions.

As always, I greatly appreciate my proofreaders; I bow so deeply to them, they've probably forgotten what my face looks like. They carefully compare the data between current and previous volumes to point out contradictions—and catch so many that somehow slipped through my own authorial check that it's frankly scary. My supervising editor suggested I should collect this sort of data into a list long, long ago...so I'm going to start figuring out ways to make editors' and proofreaders' workload lighter, little by little. *Rearguard* has about as much of this information as an RPG—and I don't have any plans to introduce new skills, equipment, or characters any less frequently. The Labyrinth Country is vast; any one of its labyrinths can produce countless monsters and items, and the Seekers who explore it are numerous and diverse.

To close this out, I'd like to return to what I said at the beginning: Thank you so, so much for your readership and support.

That's all from me for now! I hope to see you in the pages of the next volume.

With warm regards from just after the harvest moon,

Tôwa

HAVE YOU BEEN TURNED ON TO LIGHT NOVELS YET?